The Tale of
The Teller of Tales

Joshua Landsman

Pgoat Press

Published by Pgoat Press
pgoat.com

© Joshua Landsman 2015
First Pgoat Press edition 2015

Cover image by Gustave Doré: Pantagruel's Meal, from
Pantagruel by Francois Rabelais.
Catalog of tortures in chapter 4 based on *A History of Torture*
by George Riley Scott, Merchant Book Company Limited,
New edition (April 1995).

ISBN 978-0-692-51619-5

Contents

To Beth, Ellie, Claudia, Charlie—and Jerry.
Please don't be embarrassed.

The Tale of
The Teller of Tales

Prologue

"This," said the round, red-faced man to an audience of powdered and bewigged Lords and Ladies, "is…"

THE TALE OF THE MIGHTY HUNTER AND THE RAT

Once there was a mighty hunter who, like the young St. Julian the Hospitaller, sought and slew every species of creature on earth. With his colossal saw-toothed knife he slew the beasts who crept upon the ground; with his awesome bow and never-empty quiver of arrows he slew the birds who flew in the air; and with his razor-sharp harpoon he dove into the sea and slew the fishes who swam there. Like St. Julian the Hospitaller, he left in his path a mountain of corpses that climbed into the sky and glowed red in the setting sun—but unlike St. Julian, he did not in his enthusiasm accidentally kill his mother and father, so that he went on hunting day after day without remorse. In short, there was not a tiger too fearsome nor a fly too insignificant that the mighty hunger did not pause to kill.

One day as the mighty hunter passed a garbage heap on his way to the forest to slay stags, an unfortunate rat happened to catch his eye. He leapt upon the rat with his usual ferocity, and though it bit and scratched and struggled desperately, the hunter closed his fingers around its throat and began to squeeze the life out of it.

Now here it must be noted that the hunter had never found much use for God, or for those who believed in Him. What use could he, a mighty hunter, possibly have for a God who noted each sparrow that fell, or made the lion lie down with the lamb? Nor could the mighty hunter feel anything but contempt for parlor tricks such as holy statues that wept blood, or visions of blessed virgins in the sky. These were meager little miracles indeed, and they convinced the hunter that the people who were humbled by them and the God who supposed them worth performing lacked nerve and imagination. But as the hunter squeezed the rat between his iron finger and thumb, an inexplicable thing happened: the rat, who was the most miserable and reviled of all the animals, became still and spoke. In a hoarse voice it said, "I am the Lord, Your God!" — or so it seemed to the hunter — and then it died. This was not quite a visitation from Christ Himself, who appeared to St. Julian as a leper whose sores Julian warmed with his body, but it startled the hunter nonetheless, and he let the rat fall to the ground.

No longer did the hunter seek out and slay every

species of creature on earth. Instead, he sought rats exclusively, and strangled all he found as he had strangled the first. But not one of them before dying said "Boo!" let alone "I am the Lord, Your God!" and after many years of strangling too many rats to be counted the hunter himself died, not knowing whether he had really seen and heard what he thought he had seen and heard, and not knowing whether God was real.

"Well," said the round, red-faced man, "he would know the answer soon enough!" And he laughed at his own cleverness, as did the nodding Lords and Ladies, who also applauded politely.

Then a little voice said, "But what's the moral?" It came from a little girl who had snuck into the room.

"Excuse me?" said the round, red-faced man.

"Aren't fables supposed to have morals?" said the little girl.

"Indeed they are," said the round, red-faced man. "My, what a bright young lady you are. What do *you* think the moral is?"

"Um... a rat'll say anything to save its life?" said the girl.

The round, red-faced man and Lords and Ladies chuckled.

"Ah, no," said the man. "I think the moral is"—and here he puffed himself up—"those who seek proof of God's existence lack the faith to find it."

Again the Lords and Ladies chuckled and applauded while nodding. "Thank you," said the well-dusted hostess. "Your ingenious tale has entertained, instructed and uplifted us, as do all your tales. Now—to the music room!"

And as everyone followed her out, the little girl said to herself, "But if you have to have faith in it, then it isn't proof of anything... is it?"

Chapter One: To Uaxala

A celebrated Teller of Tales, known through-out the world for the ingeniousness and moral probity of his fables as well as their ability to entertain, instruct and uplift at the same time, received an invitation from a distant land—so distant that neither the Teller of Tales (who, for the sake of brevity will be referred to from now on as the Fabulist) nor his family, nor his serv-ants, nor his many connections, had ever heard of it or its King. This inclined the Fabulist to decline the invitation, for he did not like to squander his fables in places so remote that news of his tri-umphs would be unlikely to reach the rest of the world. But the King of this distant land, which was called Uaxala, had anticipated this objection, and in his invitation he promised that should the Fabulist's tales find favor with the King, as no doubt they would, the King would send criers to all the corners of the earth to proclaim the Fabu-list's greatness at length and in detail. And should by some unlikely happenstance (which could never actually happen) the tales did *not* find favor, why, Uaxala's very remoteness would prevent the rest of the world from hearing of it. This seemed quite reasonable to the Fabulist, and he resolved to go. Besides this, the King of Uaxala had also had the foresight to include with his invitation a ruby the size of his fist.

And so, one fine spring morning, the Fabulist, attended only by his Manservant, set sail on a sleek Uaxalan vessel. His wife and fourteen children waved farewell from the dock, though not nearly as forlornly as the Fabulist had expected.

"They don't seem very sad, do they?" he said to his Manservant.

"Why do you say that, sir?" said the Manservant.

"Well, look at them... they're all smiling. One would think they were happy to see me go."

"Perhaps, sir," said the Manservant, who knew his master well, "your wife is merely thinking how wonderful it is to have a husband, and your children how wonderful to have a father, whose ingeniousness and moral probity is so widely admired that Kings from lands no one has ever heard of ask him to visit."

"Hmm," said the Fabulist. "You're probably right. I hadn't thought of it that way. I am reminded of 'The Story of the Merchant and His Personal Physician.'" He went on in his most oratorical manner, "Once upon a time there was a very ill man who—"

"Excuse me, sir," said the Manservant, "but I'm feeling a little ill myself just now. Seasickness, you know. Will you be requiring anything?"

"No, I suppose not," said the Fabulist, and the Manservant fled below.

The voyage lasted many months, which the Fabulist passed by rehearsing aloud his entire repertoire of fables. None were written down in accordance with the ancient tradition that fables are meant to be heard, not read; he preferred instead to pronounce them to his Manservant. But these occasions were rare, for even after the Manservant seemed quite at home at sea, and ate his meals with relish, the poor fellow remained subject to sudden attacks of *mal de mer* whenever the Fabulist wanted to rehearse. And so the Fabulist found himself entertaining, instructing and uplifting the waves and dolphins who leapt alongside the ship. He particularly enjoyed re-visting his oldest fables, the chestnuts that had launched his career but were now so well known to every parent and child he could no longer use them to advantage. Among these were "The Husband Who Loved Garlic More than his Wife," "The Slug Who Slipped on His Own Slime," and—most well-known of all—"The Crapulous Burgomeister." Surely in far off Uaxala, isolated as it was from the common discourse of nations, these fables would enjoy renewed freshness and potency.

The Fabulist also invented new fables on the voyage. Here is an example:

THE ISLAND OF COMELY YOUNG WOMEN

A man once sailed so far and so long that he forgot about the wife who waited for him at home. On the very day she passed completely out of his memory, he chanced upon an island inhabited solely by comely young women. Naturally these women were love-starved, and they forced the man to marry all of them at once. Since each young woman longed to be the favorite with whom he would spend his time, they pampered him like a prince, not letting him perform even the simplest chores, and there arose among them a great competition in which each sought to outdo the others in bringing the man physical pleasure. Night after night they surrendered their youthful bodies to his merest whim and most lurid fantasies. Years passed in this pleasant manner, until one day he happened to remember his wife. Being a fundamentally virtuous man, he experienced a pang of guilt. But now that the comely young women were making him so completely happy, he realized how miserably his wife had failed in that very duty. And so he felt no obligation to return to her, but spent the rest of his life on the island, the moral being that wives who neglect

*their husbands will undoubtedly lose them, and right-
fully so.*

This fable, the Fabulist felt certain, would
have great appeal to husbands for its admonitory
effect on their wives. He mused upon the island
and its obliging young women day after day as
the ship sailed on through placid, sun-drenched
seas, until the fable became one of his personal
favorites.

Exactly one year to the day after embarking,
the ship reached the Uaxalan capital. Thousands
of people had come down to the waterfront to
welcome the Fabulist, and they cheered and
waved enthusiastically when he appeared on
deck. A band began to play, cannons were fired,
and white doves were released into the sky.
Nodding and smiling as he made his way down
the gangway to the dock, the Fabulist noted with
satisfaction that all of the Uaxalans wore rich
silks and plumed turbans, and on every finger
there twinkled two—if not three—gold rings
with large jewels. Even the dockhands, usually
the most disadvantaged and disreputable inhab-
itants of any country, looked clean and well fed.
Uaxala appeared to be an uncommonly wealthy
country, and the Fabulist congratulated himself
on his decision to accept the King's invitation.
Surely his visit would be especially rewarding.

A gilded open carriage pulled by six unicorns had been sent for the Fabulist, and in this he rode through the prosperous town, hailed by crowds along the way.

"What fine people," said the Fabulist to his Manservant. "What good sense they have — what an obvious appreciation for learning, virtue and invention." Awed by this welcome, the Manservant looked at the Fabulist with new eyes. But then the Fabulist said, "I cannot help recalling 'The Tale of the Rook and the Monkeys.'" He cleared his throat. "The rook had lost his way in a terrible storm and taken shelter in a tree full of..." and so on and so on, causing the Manservant to reflect that learning, virtue and invention in and of themselves might be good things, but their real goodness lay in knowing when (and when not) to display them.

The carriage came to a stop in front of a vast palace more elegant than any the Fabulist, no stranger to vast palaces, had ever seen (yet in nowise could it be called vulgar or ostentatious). He was conducted down long, hushed halls and through airy, open galleries to a splendid garden of palms and fruit trees, in the center of which was a white pavilion. Beneath this, on a pile of cushions, sat the King, surrounded by his ministers, chancellors, viziers and wizards.

Now this King was a very old man with a shining bald head, a long white beard, and bushy white eyebrows that bloomed like twin white moustaches above his eyes—yet the eyes themselves were bright and searching. In a rich, even voice he addressed the Fabulist, "At last you have come. We thank you, for we know that your voyage has been a long one, undertaken at great personal sacrifice—"

"Not at all, Your Majesty," interrupted the Fabulist. "It is I who should thank you, for inviting a humble teller of tales such as myself to visit your interesting and unknown country. Were those real unicorns that pulled my carriage, or horses with stuck-on horns?"

"Why, they're real, of course," said the King, a little startled, for he was not used to being interrupted, nor to having the genuineness of his unicorns questioned. "Are you a student of the natural sciences? I'm sure we can arrange to—"

"I'm a student of everything," said the Fabulist, "as those who walk my road in life usually are, for we weave our tales from the warp and woof of life, so to speak, the better to instruct, entertain and uplift our fellow men. As to the voyage being long, can a thinking man fail to profit from such an excellent opportunity for contemplation?"

"Quite so," said the King. "Quite true. Now—"

"I find the vast open vistas of the sea very conducive to abstract meditation, and invigorating to the imaginative faculties."

"No doubt," said the King. "In my own—"

"Shall I tell you a fable I have invented upon the waves?" asked the Fabulist. "I call it 'The Island of Comely Young Women'."

"We are all very anxious to hear it," said the King, "and no doubt we shall at the proper time. But alas, that time is not now, for we have called you to Uaxala to ask your help in dealing with a certain delicate matter."

"Indeed?" said the Fabulist.

"Yes, and if I may speak frankly and without being interrupted—"

"I beg your pardon, Your Majesty."

"If I may speak without interruption—"

"Of course."

The King sighed. "May I continue? Thank you. There is a certain troubling matter of great consequence for the future of my country, that requires—"

"I must say," said the irrepressible Fabulist, "that your country, and I have visited many, seems uniquely blessed and well-regulated."

"It was not always so," said the King. "If you had visited Uaxala fifty years ago, you would not recognize it today. Fifty years ago our country was impoverished, and our people starving and ridden with disease. Ignorance, lawlessness, moral turpitude, strife—such was the state of things fifty years ago. It is only through the good works and industry of these wise men," and here the King indicated his ministers, chancellors, viziers and wizards, "that we have been able to improve ourselves."

"Nay, beloved King," said one of the ministers, "it is you who are most responsible for our present happiness."

"Nonsense," said the King.

"It is true," said an ancient vizier to the Fabulist. "You see, the King's father had the foresight to send his son out into the world, to study at its finest universities and learn the ways of its most profound thinkers. When he returned he brought with him the best of these ways, and he has worked tirelessly ever since to apply them among us."

"God bless you," said another minister to the King, who now was blushing uncomfortably to the top of his bald head. "No sovereign has ever done so much for his people."

"Please stop," said the King. "Could one man alone accomplish what you attribute to me? Whatever I have done, you have made possible."

"Without your example and guidance," said the vizier, "we would still be knocking each other on the head to steal food from one another's mouths." And to this all the ministers, chancellors, viziers and wizards murmured their assent.

"At any rate," said the King to the Fabulist, "we have come a very long way, though we still have far to go. And that is where we hope you may help us."

"What is it you require?" asked the Fabulist. "Compelling moral insights like thunderbolts out of the blue? Inculcation of civilized values? Pedagogy disguised as entertainment?"

"Yes," said the King. "Precisely. But—"

"Then let us begin!" exulted the Fabulist, his head now quite turned (as if it needed any turning!) by these highly cultured men seeking his instruction. "There is no time like the present," he continued, "a moral suitably illustrated by 'The Tale of the Procrastinating Porker.' Once upon a time—"

"You misunderstand us, to a degree," said the King. "It is not ourselves whom we intend as your audience, although I'm sure we could all profit in that role. It is my son."

"Your son?"

"Yes, my son. The Prince." And here the King once again sighed, not from impatience as before, but from a sudden paternal heavy-heartedness. "I have followed the example of my father in sending the Prince to the same universities where I studied, but the Prince... how shall I say it? He does not seem to have benefited from the experience. It is not that he isn't bright. In fact, he completed his courses of study far more quickly than I, and mastered realms of thought quite beyond all of us. And yet... and yet... he draws from them unexpected conclusions and disputatious sophistries."

"He is cynical," said one of the ministers.

"He is hedonistic," said another.

"He behaves badly," said a third. "Forgive me, Your Majesty."

"It is true," said the King. "All of it, to our sorrow. The Prince is disrespectful of his elders, keeps low drunken company, and is profligate, having fathered bastards upon most of the palace's serving girls. Naturally this conduct makes us apprehensive about the day when he shall rule in my place—a day that is not far off, I am afraid."

"Nay, Your Majesty!" said the ministers, chancellors, viziers and wizards. "You are stronger and healthier than all of us, thanks to your hygienic scrupulosity, and you shall rule for many years yet to come!"

"But not forever, even should I wish it, which I do not," said the King. "In truth I am more tired than you know, and long for release from the burdens of state. If I could rest now knowing that Uaxala was in good hands...."

"Nay, Your Majesty, do not say such things."

"But they are so. The Prince will be King and he must be made fit."

"Yes, I have seen this before," said the Fabulist. "The Prince, from being born into privilege and prosperity without having experienced Uaxala's troubled days as you describe them, has no proper sense of his duties."

"Perhaps," said the King. "But I cannot help feeling that the source of his inexplicable behavior is something deeper and blacker and more blighting to his character."

"Then I shall blast this black spot," said the Fabulist. "I shall shine the light of truth upon it, and make it wither and fade."

"If only you could!"

"I shall; do not doubt it. The power of my fables is legendary—if I may be permitted to say so. They have reformed the criminal, healed the sick, and righted the mentally unbalanced. Why, just last year I was summoned to Moldavia where one hearing of my 'Tale of Swans on Still Waters' cured the Queen of her dropsy. And did I not bring the implacable Blackhouse Ripper to tears of repentance on the eve of his execution, so that he begged to be led to the gallows forthwith? I have fables for every occasion, and this is no exception, believe me."

"I want to believe you," said the King. "We shall see when you meet the Prince."

That night there was a great feast more sumptuous than any the Fabulist, no stranger to great feasts, had ever tucked into (he was no stranger to tucking in, either, as his ample round shape attested). He sat at the King's right hand as an unending succession of platters was presented. There was a whole roasted minotaur sauced with rosemary and lime; a hearty cassoulet of duck, white beans and whiffle-bird; jellied lion's paw; enormous golden carp steamed so slowly under wetted towels they still were gasping as they were filleted at the table; flaky spiced pies charged with tree squeak; gyascuti farsed with grebes farsed with capons farsed with wrens; and so on. The handsome Uaxalan nobility were in attendance, and they toasted the Fabulist with pale green champagnes and waters of life. Yet there was one among the nobility who was conspicuous, to the Fabulist at least, by his absence. Between courses, as the Fabulist's fingers and face were being refreshed with warm colognes, he turned to the King and asked, "Where is the Prince, Your Majesty?"

"Alas, he is most likely in a tavern," said the King. "Or worse."

"Did you not command his attendance?" said the Fabulist.

"I have long ago given up commanding him, I'm afraid."

"I see," said the Fabulist. "Does he know of my arrival, and why I have come?"

"I am sure he knows you are here, but as to why, I have not told him explicitly. It may be that he has learned it, however."

"It is no matter," said the Fabulist. "In fact, I was thinking it might be best if I were not presented to him formally, but met him under more natural circumstances—man to man you might say—or man to Prince, excuse my presumption. That way I might take his measure, gain his confidence before beginning his improvement."

"As you wish," said the King. "He rarely rises before the middle of the afternoon. If you are ready then we can... bump you into him."

"I will be ready," said the Fabulist. "I am ready now. By God, this is excellent wine!" He waved for his glass to be refilled. "Wine is the great clarifier, don't you agree? I have an excellent fable about a vineyard, about the grapes hanging heavy on the vine. Would you like to hear it?" Without waiting for an answer, he rose. "Lords and Ladies," he announced, "I am overwhelmed by your excellent hospitality and undeserved regard. Humbly and in thanks I offer a fable—what else have I to offer, being an inventor of fables? I beg you to accept it in the spirit in which it is tendered. Speaking of spirits, perhaps one more glass first." But he had overestimated his capacities, as epicureans sometimes do, and as he leaned back to down this last glass, he crashed over backwards, breaking his chair to splinters. His Manservant and the attendants who rushed forward found him to be sound asleep with a dreamy smile on his flushed sweating face. And he too did not rise before the middle of the next afternoon, when many hands pulled him from bed, abluted and dressed him quickly, and—over the protests of his Manservant—rushed him through the palace to a pair of wide wooden doors, behind which the Prince was alleged to be found. The servants who accomplished all this disappeared as suddenly as they had appeared, leaving the Fabulist alone before the doors. However, he didn't much feel like taking the Prince's measure just then. His head ached doubly—in the front from too much wine, and in the back from a nasty bump he had acquired he knew not how—and a slackness in his bowels told him that minotaur might not agree with him. Yet when he turned to creep away from the doors, the King's head appeared around a corner and whispered, "The Prince, sir—the Prince!" And so the Fabulist had no choice but to knock.

There was no response. He knocked again with the same result—or no result, as it were.

"Knock louder!" hissed the King behind him.

"Really, Your Majesty," said the Fabulist. "I don't see the need for all of this—"

"Just go in!" said the King, waving. "Go on; go in."

The Fabulist did.

He found himself in an enormous library, lined with bookshelves to the ceiling which was three stories high. Yet there was no one—least of all a Prince—in sight.

"Hello?" said the Fabulist. His voice echoed

in the great room, and inside his head as well. "Hello?" he said again. "Anyone here?" He wandered into the room, pausing now and then to pick up a book from a shelf or table. Some he remembered dimly from his own days at the university; others were in languages completely strange to him. He stopped before a bust of someone who looked very much like the King, but who lacked the King's cultured lineament. This was, he reasoned, the King's father, who had seen the need for his son to become something finer than himself. Nearby was a portrait of a beautiful young woman—more of a girl, really. Was it the King's Queen? Or his mother? She held in her arms a swaddled baby, and was looking down at it with great tenderness. Over her shoulder there appeared to be floating in the air some kind of globe made of brass, with crystal windows lit from within. Truly there was much to marvel at here in Uaxala, and the Fabulist looked forward to telling everyone at home all about it. The country's predicament would make an excellent fable, made more excellent by his own prominent role in bringing it to a happy resolution. Still, he was relieved not to have to begin resolving it this moment, for he really wasn't feeling up to snuff. He looked around for a comfortable chair in which to take a nap. It was then that he saw a young boy, no more than ten or twelve, sitting at a far table, his nose in a book.

"Excuse me," said the Fabulist. The boy looked up, quite surprised. "I'm looking for the Prince—I was told he was in here," the Fabulist went on. "Have you seen him?"

"The Prince?" said the boy.

"Yes. Have you seen him?"

The boy put a monocle in one eye and squinted with curiosity at the Fabulist. "No, I haven't," he said.

"That's odd," said the Fabulist. "I was told he was in here."

"It is odd," said the boy. "Who are you?"

"I am the Fabulist," said the Fabulist, "sent for by the King to reform the character of the Prince."

"Oh," said the boy. "I have heard of you." Then he looked back at his book.

The Fabulist approached him. He—the boy, that is—was richly dressed, like everyone in Uaxala, but on him it looked unnatural, as if he still ought to be in short pants.

"What are you reading?" the Fabulist asked. But the boy didn't answer. He seemed to have already forgotten the Fabulist. "Good book, that?" said the Fabulist. The boy looked at him, just as surprised as before.

"Yes; it's very good," said the boy.

"What is it?"

"The *Excursus* of Hermes Trismegistus. Are you familiar with it?"

"No. A romance?"

"You might say that," said the boy.

"I myself was very fond of romances at your age. Who is the hero?"

"Hmm... that's an interesting question. I suppose the hero is God."

"How charming," said the Fabulist. "The villain then must be the devil."

"No; that's God, too."

"I don't understand," said the Fabulist, a little stiffly. "How can God be a villain, unless the book is blasphemous?"

"Blasphemous?" said the boy. "I'm sure I don't know anything about that. But as for God being hero and villain simultaneously, it seems to me quite natural and expected."

"My dear boy—do your parents know you are reading such an unsuitable book?"

"My mother's dead," the boy said quietly.

"Your father then."

The boy just shrugged.

"I should like to tell you a story," said the Fabulist.

"Oh dear," said the boy. "Must I listen?"

"It will do you good," said the Fabulist. "I call it..."

THE FLAMES OF FALSE KNOWLEDGE

Once upon a time—

"I don't like stories that start 'once upon a time'," said the boy.

"Very well, then," said the Fabulist indulgently...

In a certain place at a certain time, there dwelt a young boy who loved to set fire to things. He started by making little fires with sticks and hay, but as he grew older, these no longer satisfied him, and he made bonfires, blazes and pyres. The bigger they were, the more they whetted his appetite for even larger fires, and soon he was setting fire to sheds and carts. His parents tried everything they could think of to cure him of this habit, even locking him in his room and bringing his meals to him there. But he set fire to his bed and nearly burned down the house.

"Why do you love to make fires so much?" his parents asked him.

"Because I see things in the flames," said the boy.

"What do you see?" asked his parents.

"I see freedom, release... an end to the tyranny of matter."

His parents looked at one another and sighed. They were very goodhearted and loved the boy very much, and they bonded him as apprentice to a blacksmith, hoping this might satisfy him. For a while it seemed to. He stoked the forge with vigor, and stared into its brilliant white heart. Each night he told his parents of everything he had learned from the fire that day. For instance, one night he said the fire had spoken to him of sadness. "It moaned and sighed and made mournful exhalations," he said. "But I threw on more and more fuel and worked the bellows up and down, and the fire's sadness burned so fiercely and grew so bright that its sadness became its reason for being, and in that it seemed almost joyful. This is an important lesson for life," he said. His parents shook their heads because they did not see the value of such a lesson, even if it were true. They worried about their boy, and with good reason, for one day he burned down the blacksmith shop, killing the blacksmith and his family. He was hanged for this crime and found himself before God.

"You are the boy who saw freedom in flames," said God.

"Yes," said the boy.

"Then you shall find your freedom in Hell," said God, and He consigned the boy to the flames that burn but do not consume.

The boy—the one in the library who had listened politely to the Fabulist's fable—stared at the Fabulist as if he expected him to go on.

"Well... do you see?" the Fabulist finally said.

"See what?" said the boy.

"Why, the moral, of course. The flames that the boy thought had so much to teach him—"

"You mean, that's the end?"

"Of course it's the end."

"But what happened to the boy?"

"What do you mean what happened to him?"

"Did he find his freedom?"

"Certainly not. He burned forever in excruciating, indescribable agony, all because he—"

"I don't think so," said the boy. "I think he found his freedom—freedom from the tyranny of God."

"The tyranny of *God*?" said the Fabulist, aghast.

"The tyranny of Heaven," said the boy.

"And what," said the Fabulist, "might that be?"

"Here is what happened. May I finish your story?"

The boy burned forever without being consumed, as you say, and at first it was unbearable, though of course he had no choice but to bear it. To increase his torture, God even gave him glimpses now and then of Heaven, where multitudes of worthy people sat at the hem of God's robe and worshipped Him endlessly for His goodness. This made the boy wonder if God ever gave the people in Heaven glimpses of Hell, and if He did, what did they think? Was that why they adored God so ardently, for inflicting excruciating, indescribable agony (as you say) upon the multitudes of people who weren't worthy enough for Heaven? Or maybe those in Heaven didn't care, thought the boy. Maybe God's presence was so overpowering that they saw but didn't see, saw but were not moved, or worse—saw and approved. Either way, the boy wanted none of it. He realized then that even if he had been good—even if he hadn't killed the blacksmith and his family—he would never have set one foot into Heaven, but would have flung himself headfirst into Hell. Better to burn forever with the damned, he decided, than fall at the feet of a God who demanded such slavish, self-serving adoration. In his heart the boy thanked God for the free will that allowed him to commit his evil crime, and he began to burn so fiercely and so brightly that his pain became his freedom, and in that he was truly joyful.

It was the Fabulist's turn to stare. "For shame!" he said. "For shame!"

The boy blinked behind his monocle.

"Do you believe that?" said the Fabulist. "That God is wrong to punish sinners?"

"Oh, no. Sinners must be punished, of course. But who will punish God for the sin of punishing them forever, and expecting to be praised for it?"

"Young man," said the Fabulist, "I have seen many strange things in your country, but you are the strangest of all. What is your name?"

"Hal," said the boy.

"I am going to recommend to the King—no, I am going to *insist* that you be present when I fabulate for the Prince. You must be quiet, of course, but you must promise to listen carefully, for you seem to need my correction almost as much as the Prince."

"Oh, don't worry," the boy sighed. "I shall be there."

"Until then," said the Fabulist, and he turned to leave the library. But he stopped, went back to the boy, and held out his hand. "Give me that," he said, indicating the book. The boy surrendered it meekly, with obvious reluctance. The Fabulist tucked it under his arm and strode out.

In the hall beyond the doors of the library, the King and his ministers, chancellors, viziers and wizards were waiting.

"Well?" the King said eagerly. "How did it go?"

"If you mean how did my interview with the Prince go, I am sorry to disappoint you, for there was none," said the Fabulist.

"None?" said the King. "But what happened?"

"The Prince was not within."

"Not within? But that's impossible! He went straight in from his bath!"

"Nevertheless, he was not there," said the Fabulist. "I did, however, have a somewhat disquieting discussion with a young boy who was reading this book." He held the book out to the King.

"A young boy?" said the King, not looking at the book.

"Yes. He said his name was Hal."

"You fool!" said the King. "That was the Prince!"

"The Prince?"

"Yes—Prince Harold!"

"But that boy was no older than ten... twelve at the most!"

"And what difference should *that* make?" thundered the King.

"But that *boy*? That *boy* is the keeper of low drunken company? The begetter of bastards upon serving girls?"

"I told you he was precocious, didn't I?"

"Well, I'll be," said the Fabulist.

"How did it go, then?" asked the King.

"Go?"

"Your talk with him—how did it go?"

"Oh. That," said the Fabulist. "That went... quite well. When shall I be meeting him again?"

Chapter Two: The Tragedy of the Prince's Mother and Other Stories

An interview was set for the next evening. The King and the entire court would be present, a circumstance the Fabulist ordinarily would welcome, as he loved an audience even more than food and wine, and the larger the audience the better. Yet this first *tete-a-tete* with the Prince had disconcerted him. The boy was not a dissipated, unruly lout, as the Fabulist had expected; he was clever and articulate, a nimble if unorthodox thinker—and deceitful, too. Had he not denied he was the Prince? What's more, he had taken advantage of his innocent youthful looks to catch the Fabulist off-guard. Well, tomorrow the Fabulist would be *on* his guard, and inspired by the presence of the Uaxalan nobility he would allegorize the Prince to tears, shame him down to a penitent nubbin; fill him with uncertainty and awe. After all, the Fabulist was nine times champion of the famous *Tournee du Fabulistes*, hosted annually by the lay brothers at the monastery at

Ghurkin! While the Prince... well, he was just a boy.

Nevertheless, it did not hurt to be prepared, and that night before retiring the Fabulist instructed his Manservant to nose about among the palace's staff and learn as much as he could about the Prince. What, for instance, had happened to his mother? Whom or what did he love, and what or whom did he fear? Did he speak in boastful terms of his destined ascension to the throne, or did he speak of it not at all? Intelligence of this sort was essential to selecting the most apt fables from the Fabulist's vast catalog, and to tweaking them for maximum effect when the heat of fabulating was upon him. (The ability to extemporize—to spin out imaginative tropes as the occasion suggested—this the Fabulist considered one of his greatest strengths.)

Consequently, in the morning, so that he and his Manservant might speak confidentially, the Fabulist sent away the pretty young handmaids who were serving him an unusual but delicious breakfast of cracked black pepper flavored with anise, cumin, wintergreen and malt.

"You are looking a little pale this morning," said the Fabulist to his Manservant.

"Ah, sir," said the Manservant, "I'm not a young man anymore, and I don't bounce back easily from a night like last night."

"I assume that means you were successful in

your mission."

"It wasn't easy, sir. Servants, as you know, like nothing more than to talk about their masters—myself being an exception to this rule—but this group here..." and he shook his head, "...they were a tough nut to crack. When the jug came around I had to start pretending to take my swig, or I would've—"

"But what did you learn, man, is the issue," said the Fabulist.

"Ah... that, sir." The Manservant shook his head again. "It's a strange story, and a sad one. I got it out of a toothless old crone who wouldn't speak above a whisper and kept looking around as if the palace guard were about to spring upon her at any moment."

"Good for you," said the Fabulist. "Out with it."

"Let me think now. Things got a little muddled after a while. I don't know what was in that jug but it sure had a punch...."

"By God, I shall brain you!" said the Fabulist. And here it should be noted that the Manservant really had the full story to hand; he just enjoyed giving the Fabulist a dose of his own conversational roundaboutness.

"Well, sir," said the Manservant, "if you brain me you won't get the story, now will you?"

THE TALE OF THE TRAGEDY OF THE PRINCE'S MOTHER

It seems that long ago, the King's first wife was unable to produce a royal heir. It wasn't that she was barren, for the poor woman nearly killed herself squeezing out a child every year for nineteen years, except of course for the year in which she bore triplets... but all were girls. "Undine," the King said to her, for that was her name, "I have given you plenty of opportunities to fulfill your most important duty—indeed, your only duty, now that I think about it—and yet you have failed to do so."

"And why have I failed more than you?" said Undine, who was a proud woman. "Might it not be your failure instead of mine?"

"Nonsense," said the King. "Everyone knows that the mother grows the child the way the soil grows the wheat, and if the wheat never ripens, why, it's the fault of the soil, not the farmer who sowed the seed."

"But what if the seed was bad in the first place?" asked Undine.

At this the King's ministers, chancellors, panjandrums and what-have-you's gasped, for—

"Just a minute," said the Fabulist. "How do you know that the King said this and his wife said that?"

"The crone told me, sir," said the Manservant.

"She told you in such detail?"

"Perhaps not in so many words..."

"Stick to the facts and get to the point," said the Fabulist, "and let us not forget who is the teller of tales here, and who the Manservant."

"Of course, sir. Excuse me. At any rate..."

...the King had no choice but to marry more wives. Yet these bore him only daughters as well! He kept on trying, marrying two and three wives at a time, and the entire country held its breath with each new birth, only to be disappointed when out popped another little girl. No one could believe such rotten luck, but neither could anyone change it. The court astrologers divined from the stars the most auspicious times for royal deposits; the King's physicians bathed the wives in waters charged with the magical root of the mandrake (though this practice was discontinued for fear of spontaneous homunculi); why, the King even submitted to having his stool examined, and the wives wore boy-charms in their love-pots.

"You're making that up!" said the Fabulist.

"I'm not, sir—I swear!" said the Manservant. "That's how the old crone told it, with the stool and the love-pots and all!"

And yet it was all in vain. The palace was filling up with happy little princesses, and the country was becoming desperate. A blood-heir to the man who had led them out of savagery was considered essential, but

the King was getting old and who knew how much
longer he'd be able to rise to the occasion? As a last
extreme measure, every unmarried high-born Uaxalan
female who was old enough for monthlies and yet not
too old for them, was brought to the palace where the
King loved them all, one after the other... and then
again in reverse order, for luck. Oh it was grueling
work, especially for the King who was not by nature a
sensualist. He ate oysters till his ears rang and grew
thin and pale from loss of fluid. And it was futile
work, too, for nine months later thousands of princesses began to be born, with not a prince among them. "Is
there no woman in my entire kingdom who can bear
me a son?" cried the King in despair, and his ministers, chancellors, et cetera, met to consider what to do
next.

Some thought the wives were enchanted and
wanted to consult with witches. Others called for
witches, too, but for the purpose of fashioning a golem,
a waxwork that could be animated with a portion of
the King's own life essence.

"Can such a thing be done?" asked the in-
credulous Fabulist.

"If it could be done anywhere, that would be
here," said the Manservant.

But while all this arguing was going on, a squire
from a remote corner of the country appeared at the
palace, bringing with him his only daughter, whose

name was Toothsome. She was a shy girl of fourteen who had never been away from her home. Yet beautiful was she, and so modest and gentle and good, that the King instantly fell in love with her, which had not been the case with any of his other wives. Perhaps this was the missing ingredient, for nine months later, on the night of the vernal equinox, at the stroke of midnight, Toothsome bore him a strong, healthy boy! With tears in his eyes, the King carried his son out onto a balcony of the palace below which thousands of his subjects were waiting. He lifted the Prince into the air for all to see, and a great cheer rose up that shook the palace to its foundations and blew the leaves off trees for miles around. At last, the succession was assured; Toothsome was exalted as a saint and a savior, and the entire country rejoiced.

All, that is, except for Undine and the other wives. They had seen how the King doted on his favorite during her pregnancy, suffering terribly with her slightest discomfort, delighting in her every smile or laugh (which were frequent because of her sweet nature), and talking with her intimately such as he had never done with his other wives—not even Undine, who had borne him twenty-one daughters. Now Undine and all the rest would be forgotten, and their daughters would be slighted, and they were bitter as only cast-off women can be. Their resentment grew as the Prince grew, for it was clear from the start he was an exceptional boy. At one, he could spell "incorrigible"; at two, he foretold an earthquake; and at three, he

beat the King at chess. He seemed also to have inherit-
ed his mother's fine qualities—how could he have not,
seeing how wisely and well she loved him? He was
humble yet confident, brave yet judicious, honest yet
considerate of the feelings of others. In short, he was
everything the King and the country had hoped for,
and the rest of the wives hated him. They poisoned
their daughters against him, too.

"Isn't that the way of women?" said the Fabulist. "They are ruled by self-interest, with no
thought for the greater good."

"It gets worse, sir," said the Manservant.
"Just listen...."

Out of spite, the other wives sought to discredit
the Prince and his mother. They whispered about that
she had been already pregnant when she was brought
to the Palace, and used trickery to deceive the physi-
cians. (You see, other women had tried to advance
themselves in this way, and so all candidates were pre-
examined, not just for signs of disease but also of
pregnancy.) But no one who had seen the Prince and
King together could believe this because the two looked
so much alike. Besides, it was plain to all that Tooth-
some was incapable of even the most harmless white
lie. Nevertheless, the King was furious at his wives for
this slander, and he threatened to banish the lot of
them. But Toothsome pleaded with him not to. She
was keenly aware of the position of the other wives, as

she had inadvertently been the cause of it, and she felt sorry for them. Woe to Toothsome for her kind-heartedness, for nothing more increases the rancor of our enemies than showing them more mercy than they are capable of themselves. Toothsome might still be alive today if the King had not let himself be persuaded by her.

Now, Toothsome and Prince Hal spent most of the day together, for though the boy had forty-nine tutors, seven for each day of the week, he much preferred to read his lessons aloud to his mother, who craved learning almost as much as he did. They sang songs together, too, and played games that made them both laugh. One of their favorites was Creep and Peep, which they played in the palace's garden labyrinth, and is the Uaxalan version of our own Hide and Seek. When the Prince was eight, the King went away on a journey, and the wives saw their chance to carry out a mean prank. Undine, who held a senior position among the other wives, not just because she was the first of all, but because she most hated innocent Tooth-some, sent her daughters to the Prince, to give him a vial with a potion they said would render him invisible for a short time. "Drink this," they told him, "when you are inside the labyrinth, and your mother will never be able to find you." The Prince, of course, did not at first believe them, for his half-sisters had never been nice to him before, and besides he had read in the Chema of Chemes that the recipe for invisibility had been lost many centuries ago when the island of At-

lantis sank. But the daughters staged a demonstration in which one of their number appeared to sip from the vial, upon which she disappeared in a puff of smoke. (She had exploded the smoke herself and run away behind it.) The rest of the daughters pretended she was still among them, pushing and tripping them invisibly while she laughed and threw her voice from her hiding place. The Prince was delighted, for despite his early accomplishments, he was playful at heart and not yet as worldly as events were about to make him. He took the vial and went to find his mother for a game. Once inside the labyrinth, he drank from the vial, but instead of disappearing, he fell stiffly to the ground.

"The she-devils!" said the Fabulist. "Had they poisoned him?"

"In a sense," said the Manservant. "For although he remained fully conscious and still could see and hear…"

…the potion had paralyzed him so completely that even his heart and breathing appeared to have stopped. The poor boy was terrified, naturally, but try as he might to move or cry out, he could not. All he could do was wait for his mother to find him, yet his fears were doubled because he thought he was invisible as well as paralyzed, and then how would his mother ever find him unless she tripped over him? Trembling throughout his body—that is, he would have been trembling if he had been able to move—he lay in the

grass and listened for his mother's footstep. "Come out, come out," he heard her calling distantly, then closer and closer. Then he heard a gasp, and her stricken face appeared above him. "Dear Hal," she cried, "what's wrong?" And when he did not respond to her attempts to rouse him, she whispered, "God in Heaven! He's dead!" She clasped him to her and wept so piteously he almost wished he were dead, not to hear it. Her cries brought her attendants, and they brought a doctor who held a mirror to the Prince's nostrils, listened for his heart, and stuck him all over with a needle (which hurt quite a bit, and yet he could not say "ouch"). The doctor shook his head and gravely closed the Prince's eyelids. At this Toothsome swooned away, was revived and swooned again when she saw the Prince, and the two of them were carried to the palace—the mother limp as a noodle and the son stiff as a board.

Word spread quickly that the Prince was dead and his mother was inconsolable. This was the worst disaster imaginable, and the entire palace, who loved them both dearly, were overcome with sorrow. Except, of course, for the King's other wives and their daughters—even the littlest ones!—who exulted in secret in their chambers. Yet when night had come and the Prince had not recovered, Undine grew a little afraid, as she had not expected the effects of the potion to last so long. Alas, she had miscalculated; the Prince's young body was too small for the dose she had brewed. Meanwhile, Toothsome was raving like a madwoman.

She would cry and laugh in the same breath, tear her clothes and claw at herself, talk happily to the Prince as if nothing at all had happened to him, then fall silent and stare out the window.

That night, she wandered like a wraith through her chambers. The next day, she sat motionless beside the Prince, who had been laid out to await the return of the King. She said nothing all day, not giving any indication that she heard her attendants' pleas to come away and rest. Meanwhile, the Prince's heart was breaking. Toothsome had opened his eyes so that he might look still alive, and each time her face came into view, he could barely recognize it, so changed was she by grief and despair. If only he could blink or produce a tear, to let her know he was not dead! But the potion still held him in its fiendish grip. Then he began to think that perhaps he was dead, after all. Perhaps death was not loss of life, but merely this loss of the ability to participate in it. Soon he would be buried or burned on a bier, all the while remaining horribly aware of it. This thought chilled his soul, and he gave himself up to hopelessness. But then he caught sight of his desolated mother, and all consideration of his own plight left him. His thoughts were for her alone.

Darkness came. Toothsome disappeared from his side, and minutes passed that seemed like hours. During this time, the Prince tried methodically to move each part of his body, from his tongue to his fingertips to his toes. He felt as if he were struggling against a great wind or tide, or attempting to cast off a *great weight. It seemed futile, and yet... there! He succeeded in moving his eyes, for the potion was wearing off at last! At that moment, he heard his mother return. His heart leaped with joy. Surely she would see him looking at her, and realize he wasn't dead. She stood above him for a long while, gazing down at him mournfully, and he rotated his eyes in their sockets. But the room was too dark for her to see it. She bent down and kissed him, whispered, "No mother should outlive her child," and drew a golden dagger from her robes. "No!" the Prince tried to scream to no avail. Toothsome gripped the dagger and pointed it at her heart. "NO!" the Prince tried again, and this time the word burst from his lips. But it was too late. The dagger was flying home, and though in the instant before it struck, Toothsome heard her son cry out and realized her mistake, she was unable to hold it back. The dagger plunged deep into her breast, and she fell dead across the Prince.*

The Fabulist shuddered. "How horrible," he said.

"Indeed," said the Manservant.

The King returned several days later, by which time the Prince had recovered from the potion. Tearfully, he told his father how he had been tricked, and how it led to his mother's death, and the King went into seclusion for a week. When he emerged he exiled his wives and their daughters to a secret island in the middle of the ocean. If they ever left it they would be hunted down and killed, as would anyone who ever set foot there.

"My Island of Comely Young Women!" said the Fabulist.

"How's that, sir?" said the Manservant.

"Never mind. Go on."

"There's not much more to tell. Since then, the Prince has fallen ever deeper into cynicism, misanthropy and rebellion."

"Who can blame him?"

"They say he is haunted by his mother's expression as she died learning he yet lived. And he is especially troubled by the fact that his mother was a suicide. For according to the teachings of the Uaxalan church, no suicide can enter into heaven—not even the good and innocent ones, who kill themselves by mistake."

"Hmm," said the Fabulist. "That sheds light on our little talk yesterday."

"In what way?" said the Manservant.

"Clearly, the Prince is at war with the world and its creator."

"What do you think, then? Can you help him?"

"I must try; it is my duty. For though the ways of God to men may be mysterious, we must become reconciled to His wisdom."

"Well, I certainly hope you can reconcile the

Prince, sir, because last night I heard something else you should know."

"What is that?"

"A *valet de chambre* overheard the King telling the Captain of the Guard to prepare a pillory."

"A pillory!"

"Yes, sir. Apparently the King is disappointed in you so far, and he said that if you continue to cavort like a fool—"

"A fool!"

"I'm just repeating what the valet said the King said, sir. He said that if you continue to cavort like a fool, he will paint you yellow, lock you in a pillory, and send you home that way."

"But he can't do that!"

"I don't see why not, sir. I recommend caution."

"Caution! Who are you to recommend caution to *me*!"

"Please, sir, for both of our sakes—"

"I am not cautious! I am bold! I strike out! I overcome!"

"But sir—"

"Get out," said the Fabulist. "Go back to your valets de chambre and your crones." But when his Manservant had left, he did not feel quite so bold or overcoming. He felt alone and very far from home, with nothing but his wits to get him back. "Well, I've come a long way to

learn a valuable lesson," he said to himself.
"Never trust a king, no matter how condescending he may seem. In fact, a condescending king
may be the sort one should trust least of all!" He
paced back and forth, pondering the story he had
just heard but not seeing how to remedy its dev-
astating effect on the Prince. "This is knotty," he
thought. "This is more than I expected." If there
were a remedy he would have to find it quickly.
So he retired to the privy to stink and think. This
method had served him well in the past. But
while the stinking proceeded nicely, the thinking
did not. Suppose, for example, that an idea began
to stir deep within his mind, while simultaneously a stirring began in his bowels. At this stage, it
was too early to tell if the idea would develop
into a full fable, or, as was possible with the
lower rumblings, would prove to be more air
than earth. In fact, he could not yet even say what
the idea was, and so he bore down in opposite
directions, toward the head and toward the tail,
in a dual effort to give shape and substance to the
brute matter originating in each. Despite some
mental and abdominal cramping, the Fabulist
grew hopeful, for he felt in his gut a reassuring
heaviness tending downward, even as there arose
before his mind's eye the image of a headstrong
young bee who thumbs his feelers at everything
and everyone in his orderly community—
including his mother the Queen and his father,

her royal consort. (The Fabulist felt this inversion of mother-father roles was ingenious). Gradually, the fable divided itself into a beginning, a middle, and an ending, just as his stool did form into leading and trailing sections. As the sections traveled southward, the Fabulist began to feel the point (the point of the fable, that is), specifically: the young bee learns a painful lesson which impresses upon him the importance of honoring and obeying one's parents, and by extension the Parent of us all. But *how* would that lesson be driven home? What event making clever use of seemingly innocuous details from earlier in the fable would satisfactorily tie off the entire movement? Would the young bee become lost far from the hive? Would he sip from a forbidden poisonous flower? The Fabulist knew that the success or failure of the fable turned entirely upon this particular, for should the fable not finish up with the proper roundness and finality of form—should he have to force the issue to a conclusion—some stray clinging fragments might be left behind, for the Prince to call attention to and mock. Adjusting himself on the privy seat, the Fabulist prepared for the simultaneous delivery his creations... and yet something had gone wrong. The solidity he was hoping for announced itself loudly as nothing but a great gust of wind, and the Fabulist realized the fable of the bee was too simplistic and direct for a cynic of the

Prince's stripe. The Fabulist sagged with disappointment and fatigue. Now he would have to begin all over again. After a moment's rest, he girded himself for the effort.

At lunchtime, when the pretty handmaids reappeared with sausages and cheeses and *flèche de lard*, they did not find the Fabulist in his rooms. They left his lunch, but not a bite of it had been eaten when they returned after several hours to massage him. They were relieved, for they were afraid he would expect more of them than this simple healthful service, and none were eager for that. But as they were leaving, they heard fearful blasts from the privy. This made them giggle, and covering their pretty mouths with their hands, they approached the privy door to listen. From inside came further detonations, accompanied by groans, sighs, rude grunts, and forceful oaths. Just then, the Manservant came in, and the handmaids fled like twittering doves, their thin gowns fluttering about them. The Manservant also listened at the privy, then said through the door, "Making progress, sir?"

"Don't be impertinent," said the Fabulist from within.

"May I get you anything?"

"A basin of water."

This, the Manservant fetched, but he hesitated to carry it in. "Shall I leave it here for you?" he asked.

"Just set it inside the door."

The Manservant cracked the door open, and out came such noxious smells as arise from bubbling pits of sulfur. He slid the basin in on the floor and quickly pulled the door to. After a moment, the Fabulist appeared. His face was ashen and sweaty. "Where have you been?" he asked.

"In the gardens," said the Manservant. "They are most uncommonly peaceful, sir—and you should hear the songbirds!"

"I'm so glad you have been enjoying yourself while I have been struggling to save our skins."

"But you sent me away."

"That's no excuse," said the Fabulist, and he sat down and began eating in silence.

"Have you found your inspiration, sir?" said the Manservant.

"You'd better hope I have," said the Fabulist, in a grumble that made it clear he had not. The Manservant was tempted to say something about only one pillory being prepared, not two. But he thought better of it, for he knew that, should the Fabulist be sent home in disgrace, he would soon be looking for another situation. Despite the Fabulist's platitudinous ponderosity, being his Manservant was not all bad—and besides, the Manservant was fond of the Fabulist the way one is fond of a useless clumsy dog one has kept for a long time.

"You know, sir, I did some thinking in the gardens," said the Manservant.

"Heaven help us," said the Fabulist.

"Actually, I was thinking about something you once said to me." At this the Fabulist stopped chewing and looked up. The Manservant continued. "It was many years ago, before you had become as famous and respected as you are now. You said, 'A man never gets as far as when he doesn't know where he is going.'"

"I did say that, didn't I?" said the Fabulist. "That's quite good."

"It is, sir, and I've never forgotten it."

The Fabulist narrowed his eyes. "So what's your point?" he said.

"Just that you ought not to worry so much in advance about what to say to the Prince. You ought to trust your instincts. Perhaps let the Prince reveal himself first, then react with your natural perspicacity."

The Fabulist considered. "You may be right," he said at last.

"I'm sure of it, sir," said the Manservant. "You can't help but penetrate to the core of things this way. It's your nature."

"But then again, you may be wrong," said the Fabulist, and he resumed eating. Into his mouth went the last bit of sausage, and down his throat went the last of a tankard of cock-ale. Then he rose and returned to the privy. And there he remained for the rest of the afternoon, splitting the air with thunderous thunderclaps and sending forth great plumes of gas. It was only at sunset, when the pigeons were returning to the palace's many towers and minarets, that he emerged.

"Dress me," he said to his Manservant. "I am ready."

The feast that night made the one that had welcomed the Fabulist to Uaxala look paltry. Whereas before there had been a minotaur, now there were a dozen—a remarkable number even for Uaxala which was home to most of the world's remaining minotaurs, yet not so many that they might be roasted and eaten extravagantly; and whereas before the gyascuti had been farsed with grebes farsed with capons farsed with wrens, now the farsing did not stop there, for inside the wrens were baby bush tits, and inside the bush tits were finches, and inside the finches were hummingbirds farsed with currants. To this were added a great many other exotic and succulent dishes, and dining upon them were dukes and grand dukes, counts and viscounts, barons, baronets, marquis and earls—and, of course, their respectively-titled wives as well. All were expecting the Prince to make a colossal monkey out of the Fabulist, as he had made monkeys out of most of them at one time or another, and none wanted to miss it. Nor did they want to miss seeing the Fabulist painted yellow and clapped into a pillory, for word of the King's displeasure had spread. They watched the Fabulist closely during the meal... yet if he had any idea of what was in store for him, he gave no sign of it. He ate and drank as much as before, laughed and over-bore just as much and just as loudly, and in general acted like a man who was among great friends who loved and admired him. So much the better, thought the Uaxalans with relish. Now if only the Prince would oblige them by showing up.

More than once during the meal the King sent pages to fetch the Prince from his chambers, yet they returned each time saying he was not there.

"Go to the taverns and the gaming houses then," said the King. "Find him wherever he is and bring him here."

"Perhaps he is afraid to match wits with me," said the Fabulist as he raised a glistening oyster on a skewer to appraise it.

The King appraised the Fabulist. "I have never known the Prince to be afraid to match anything with anyone," he said. "It's more likely he thinks you are not worth the trouble."

"As indeed I am not," said the Fabulist, "for who am I but a fat foolish storyteller—a figure of fun, as it were, whose stories may be suitable for young children and old women, but not for serious-minded men?"

"The world does not seem to think of you that way," said the King.

"No, it does not," admitted the Fabulist. "But then, Uaxala is not like the rest of the world."

At this the King felt a sudden compassion for the Fabulist, who, after all, had not had to come all the way to Uaxala merely to be humiliated and discredited. Perhaps in his desperation to reach his son, the King was expecting the Fabulist to accomplish the impossible, in an impossibly short time. He had not meant for the meeting of the Prince and the Fabulist to be a sort of contest, yet somehow it had turned into one. And even should the Fabulist outshine the Prince, what good would come of that?

"My dear sir," said the King, "you must forgive me—"

At that moment, the doors to the great hall flew open, and in stumbled the Prince. He was clearly drunk and the company fell silent. He looked about, squinting through his monocle (which, if the Fabulist recalled correctly, he had been wearing in the other eye the day before), and spying a wineglass on a nearby table he scooped this up and drank it down at once. He took another and drank it too, and another and another. Then he burped loudly (the company tsked and tutted) and wiped his mouth on his sleeve. "That's better," he said. "Now where's my father?" All eyes turned toward the head of the hall, where the King sat with his face averted. "Oh... there you are," said the Prince, and he made his way unsteadily toward him, stopping now and then to empty more wineglasses and leer at all the duchesses, countesses, baronesses, marquesas, et cetera—even the very old and very ugly ones. As he did so, the Fabulist tried to reconcile his appearance with that of the boy from the library, for although he still looked quite young, he had none of yesterday's innocence and bookishness. His eye was the oblique one of the habitual drunk, his mouth was set at a hard weary slant, and his hand trembled slightly as he reached for more wine. These details touched the Fabulist's heart even through the many layers of fat that protected it, and the evening was cast in a new light. Like the King, the Fabulist now saw it less as a contest for oratorical glory, and more as a struggle to save a troubled boy's soul. He would have to proceed even more artfully than he had anticipated, for saving a soul was far more difficult than being clever at someone else's expense—and far more important.

The Prince now stood before the King. "Excuse me for being late, father," he said. "I had meant to be here to please you, but not having the fear of God before my eyes, I went to visit a whore. Even so, I should have had plenty of time, and yet she would not oblige me. I pleaded with her, flattered her, and tried to bribe her, but she resisted my efforts stoutheartedly. 'Damn it, woman!' I cried. 'Will you submit or not?'

"'Nay, your Royal Highness, do not ask me!' said she.

"'But why not?' said I. 'You have submitted many times before.'

"'Aye sir, that is true,' said she, 'but I have been with your father not three hours ago!'"

The company gasped and the King shot up from his chair in anger. "Enough!" he said. "I fear I have been far too patient with—"

But the Fabulist burst out in loud laughter. "By God, that's a good one!" he shouted.

"Thank you," said the Prince, a little surprised.

"'Been with your father three hours ago!'" said the Fabulist, his round belly bouncing as he laughed. "'Nay sir, do not ask me!' That's a good one!" He dabbed at his eyes with a corner of the tablecloth.

The King, still enraged, his bald head glowing hotly, turned upon the Fabulist. "And you, sir!" he said. "That you of all people should encourage him!"

"Oh, don't be such a wet blanket," said the Fabulist. "The boy made a good joke, even if you were the butt of it." The King stared at him in astonishment. "Let's all have a laugh and show

how big we can be," the Fabulist went on. "Sit down."

"Sit down?" said the dumbfounded King.

"Yes, sit down. Go on; sit." And here, as a sign, he jerked his eyes sideways at the King's chair, while beneath the table he actually kicked the King in the ankle.

"Ow!" said the King. But he glanced at the Prince and sat as he'd been told.

A murmur ran through the hall. Never before had the Prince been so brazen with his father, and though the King was not overly formal, never had anyone been as familiar with him as the Fabulist had just dared to be. If the evening continued along these lines, the company whispered amongst itself, surely before it was over the pillory would be rebuilt into a gallows.

In a corner of the hall, the Manservant overheard this whispering and swallowed nervously.

Meanwhile, the Fabulist was addressing the Prince:

"Dear Hal—I may call you Hal, mayen't I?" asked the Fabulist. "I have been giving yesterday's interview considerable thought."

"So we all have smelled," said the Prince, and there was a little laughter around the hall.

The Fabulist laughed, too. "I see you have gotten wind of my methods," he said, "if I may be permitted to make a little joke of my own." But no one laughed. "I admit they are odd, and yet they are productive."

"Does that mean I shall have to listen to another fable?" asked the Prince.

"That is what your father has brought me all the way to your country for," said the Fabulist.

"And yet you are such an ass..." the Prince began, and the company laughed again, although to their credit there was a reproachful noise or two.

The King pounded his fist upon the table and said to his son, "I insist you at least be civil!" But the Fabulist motioned for him to be quiet.

"You are such an inflated windbag," continued the Prince, "such a pompous, blustering know-nothing who does not hesitate to parade his ignorance at every opportunity, that apparently my father now regrets it."

"And yet I do not," said the Fabulist, "for I have seen many wonders here and feel there is much to learn from your ways."

"If that is so," said the Prince, "perhaps I ought to tell *you* a story."

"I wish you would. In fact... I was going to suggest that very thing. I have always said, a teller of tales must keep his ears and eyes open at all times, the better to—"

"Then do shut up," said the Prince, "so I may tell it."

"I beg your pardon," said the Fabulist.

"Thank you," said the Prince. He drank more

wine and closed his eyes. He remained like this for quite a long time, appearing to be deep in thought, while the Fabulist, the King, and the entire company waited for him to begin. But slowly his head tilted backward, his mouth fell open, and it was noted with some embarrassment that he was snoring.

"Hal," said the King; then "Hal!" again, louder.

The Prince awoke with a start. "What's that?" he said and looked about uncertainly.

"You were going to tell us a story," said the Fabulist.

"Of course," said the Prince. "A story. What about?"

"We don't know," said the Fabulist. "You haven't told us yet."

"Ah. Yes. I was merely waiting for *you* to pick the subject," said the Prince. "Pick any subject you wish, and I will dilate upon it with such withering skill and originality that ever after you will hesitate to peddle your own paltry tales, so piss-poor will they seem in comparison."

"Harumph," said the Fabulist. "I don't know about that, but very well: I choose as the subject God's greatness, His goodness; His justness in dealing with men, and His infinite mercy towards their failings."

The Prince belched again, having just finished off another glass of wine.

"It's a fine subject, don't you think?" said the Fabulist. "You might say it's the *only* subject, for every story in heaven and on earth is also about God in an ultimate sense."

"All right then," said the Prince. "Listen carefully. I call this story..."

THE TALE OF THE BOY AND HIS BELOVED

Once upon a time...

(The Prince smiled at the Fabulist.)

...there were a boy and a girl who were more in love than any two people had ever been before. That's what they believed, at any rate. They decided to marry, yet on the very morning of their wedding the girl fell ill and the doctor told the boy she might linger for a while, but would certainly die.

"But that can't be," said the boy. "She can't die—you mustn't let her."

"I'm afraid there's nothing I can do," said the doctor. "She's in the hands of God." And so the boy spent all day at her bedside, kissing her limp fevered hand, and all night he spent in the church, not sleeping a wink but kneeling before the altar and praying the entire time. "Dear God," he prayed, "who is just and merciful beyond our understanding, please spare my beloved and restore her to me. If You do this, I promise to hoist this great altar upon my back and

roam our vast country telling every single soul who lives in it how great and good You are. I swear I will not rest until this is done, if only You will spare my beloved." And God must have heard him, for after seven days and nights of this vigil, the girl opened her eyes and smiled at the boy.

"I don't understand it," said the doctor. "No one has ever recovered from this fever before."

"God has worked a miracle, as I knew He would," said the boy. Then he told his beloved of his promise to God and bade her farewell for now, though it pained him greatly to do so.

"Hurry back, my love," she called to him from her sickbed as he went out the door.

"I will," he said. "God will make my feet fly over the ground! I'll be back before you know it!" He went straight to the church to fetch the altar, but as he stood before it, he could not help quailing at his promise, for in daylight he saw how large the altar was, and that it was made of heavy marble and gold. Yet a promise is a promise, especially one made to God, and with the help of the priest he managed to hoist the altar onto his back. His legs bowed under its weight, his knees cracked, and his back felt as if it would break.

"Can you walk?" asked the priest.

"Urk!" came the boy's voice from beneath the altar, which was so huge it hid him from sight.

"Perhaps God would not mind if you took the smaller altar from the chapel," said the priest.

"N-No," said the boy, "it must be this one, for

that is what I p-pledged to God."

"But it's impossible!" said the priest. "You will kill yourself!"

"God will give me strength," said the boy, and he staggered with the altar toward the door of the church.

"Look out!" said the people who had gathered outside to watch. "Here he comes!"

Down the steep steps came the boy and the altar, and at the bottom he stopped to catch his breath. Already his muscles burned like fire, and sweat was pouring from his face and back. Steeling himself, he called out, "God is great! God is good! My beloved was dying but God worked a miracle and restored her!"

A great cheer rose up from the people.

"Now I go to spread the news," said the boy, and he trudged out of the village, the altar swaying upon his back. To all those he met along the way, he proclaimed: "God is great! God is good! My beloved was dying but God worked a miracle and restored her!"

Now, the country in which this happened (for it really did happen, you know) is very large, and were it flat as a pancake it would take years to walk from one end to the other. But it is also very mountainous, and by a trick of physics most of the mountains go up on one side yet do not come down on the other — on the other side they go up, too!

"Ha!" said the Fabulist. "You have done your tale a disservice there, for who can believe that a mountain goes up on the other side too!"

"It is strange, I admit," said the Prince, "and yet not unprecedented. Think of the very top of a world that is round, like a ball, where whichever way one faces is south. And what about the very center of such a world? There, every direction is up!"

"A round world, indeed," said the Fabulist. "Ridiculous. But go on."

"Thank you..."

One can see then, that in carrying the altar and his message of hope to every corner of the country, the boy's way was always uphill, and to make matters worse the weather was abominable, for that is the only kind of weather they have there. When the sky wasn't dumping torrents of rain onto the boy, it was heaping upon him cartloads of snow or driving harsh sleet or hail into his face. On those rare days when the sun did shine, it was mercilessly hot and oppressive. Thus, the ground was either a quagmire of mud, a treacherous sheet of ice or a burning desert, or was buried beneath drifts of snow—and the wind blew so fiercely from whichever direction he was heading that on some days he went more backwards than forwards. And yet his resolve did not weaken. Day after day, from dawn till dusk, he staggered from village to village, calling out from beneath the altar that "God is great! God is good! My beloved was dying but God worked a miracle and restored her!" To all who asked who he was and why he was breaking his back under such a heavy load, he patiently told the whole story of his beloved's illness and his promise to God. Upon hearing this, most people honored him, and threw him whatever slops the pigs had not eaten so that he might not go hungry, or let him sleep on the dung heaps behind their huts. (Some, though not all, were even thoughtful enough to wait until he had arisen to add to the dung heaps.) Likewise, they were very helpful in letting him know about any hermits or recluses who lived in remote places such as mountain-top aeries and inaccessible caves, for they knew that to fulfill his covenant with God he would have to visit them all. The boy thanked these people for their kindness, which he rightly interpreted as yet another sign of God's mercy.

Some people, however, were mocking and cruel. "Hey altar boy!" they called after him. "What village did you say you were from? I think I'll go there and keep your girl warm while you're away!" Such taunts stung the boy, especially when his spirits were low, which was often. He hated that altar more than he could say, hated his country for being so large, and sometimes he cursed himself for making such a foolish rash promise to God, even though it had been necessary to save his beloved's life. Then her face would appear on a cloud, or in a pool of still water, and she would smile upon him with such love and devotion that he was freed from all doubt. The altar would grow light as a feather, and he looked forward to the day when he could return to his village and marry his beloved at last.

Years passed. The boy was now a man who walked slowly and was bent over even when he had laid down the altar. His skin was like leather from his hardy way of life, and on his face there was a long ragged beard that made him appear much older than he was. One day he entered a village that looked famil-iar to him, so that he feared it was one he had already visited. Still, he had passed through so many that looked alike he could not be sure, and he dared not skip this one for fear of breaking his promise (which, if you remember that far back, was to proclaim God's good-ness and greatness to every soul in the land). He stopped at a cottage to beg some water, and when he knocked at the door a woman answered.

"God is great! God is good!" he said to her as he set down the altar. "My beloved was dying but God worked a miracle and restored her!"

"How nice of Him," said the woman. "Would you like something to eat?"

"Praise God, yes," said the man. The woman went into the cottage and came back with bread and figs. Several children followed behind her, and they looked with great curiosity at the man. They ran playfully between his bowed legs, and playfully tugged at his beard.

"Have you come a long way?" asked the woman.

"Oh yes," said the man. "I am a mendicant criss-crossing our vast country to thank God and praise Him for the goodness He has shown us—my beloved

and me, I mean."

"You must love her quite a lot."

"I do. And she loves me."

"Have you been away from her long?"

"Years."

"She must miss you terribly," asked the woman.

"And I miss her. But my absence has only made our love stronger, and we will be that much happier when we are united."

"Tell me your story,' said the woman, and the man did. He told her how his beloved had been stricken by a fever on the very morning of their wedding, and how he spent many days at her bedside and many nights in the church, not sleeping a wink but praying the entire time. He told her of his promise to God and how his beloved miraculously recovered. As he spoke, the woman's smile grew wide. At last she could no longer contain her laughter.

"No!" she said. "Is it really you?"

"Who?" said the man, not understanding.

"Is it really you?" said the woman again. "The boy I was to marry?"

The man peered at her. "Can it be?" he whispered. "Are you... are you my beloved?"

"I am," said she, "or I was, at least."

"And these children," said the man. "Whose are they?"

"They're mine, of course!"

"But who... who is their father?"

"Why, my husband!"

"*Your* husband*!*"

"*Who else?*"

"*But that means,*" wailed the man, "*you didn't wait for me?*"

"*Wait for you?'* laughed the woman. "*You disappeared long ago!*"

"*I didn't disappear! I was fulfilling my promise to God!*"

"*But how was I supposed to know? You never sent word to me—not once! For all I knew you had been crushed by that alter or eaten by wolves, or had used that stupid promise as an excuse to run away without marrying me. I never dreamed you were still carrying that altar around, telling everyone how great and good God is! Who could be dumb enough to do a thing like that?*"

The man sank to the ground. His beloved (for to him that is what she still was, even though she had forgotten him) knelt beside him. "You poor boy," she said tenderly, wiping dirt from his face. "You broke my heart going off like that, but now I see how fortunate I was not to have married you after all."

"*It's true,*" *said the man.* "*I'm an idiot.*" *And he never rose from that spot, but died right there beside the altar.*

Now, the Uaxalan aristocracy usually favors humility before God to hubris, yet most could not suppress their delight in the Prince's story, so clever was the telling and so provocative the moral. Some laughed, some said "Well done!" and others even applauded. But this caused the King to glower until all fell silent with lowered eyes. The Prince, who was gulping down still another glass of wine, seemed not to notice his father's displeasure—and the Fabulist, too, was ignoring the King and looking instead at the Prince, as if waiting for him to continue.

"And then what happened?" asked the Fabulist.

"Excuse me?" asked the Prince.

"What happened next? For certainly that isn't the end."

The Prince struck his forehead. "Oh yes, of course," he said. "How stupid of me. I forgot the part in which the man went to heaven where his brow was anointed with soothing balsams by the angels, who sang hosannas to his faithfulness forever and ever, and God allowed him to sniff at His heels like the good little lapdog he was until in the fullness of eternity the dreadful ordeal he had endured on Earth was forgotten by him, or remembered as lasting not years and years but only the briefest portion of a second." The Prince smiled. "Is that better?"

"Why, er… quite," said the Fabulist, but in truth it was not, for this was precisely how the Fabulist had determined to usurp the Prince's story, much as the Prince had usurped *his* story in the library. What was more, the Fabulist saw that by usurping his usurpation before he had the chance to usurp, the Prince had unintentionally saved him further embarrassment, or rather embarrassed him slightly less than he (the Fabulist, that is) would have embarrassed himself by uttering it. No doubt he would have painted this ending in nobler colors than had the Prince—lapdog of God indeed!—yet even so, it would have swayed the Prince not at all, and fallen abysmally flat before the company.

Was the Fabulist so rattled that he had lost his wits entirely? Apparently this was the case and more, for the Fabulist now found himself at an extremity which he knew of only from the accounts of other men, because never before had he experienced it, not even as a youth nor as a child. Specifically: he had not a word to say! Every eye in the hall (including the Prince's) was upon him; the King watched him with an expression that managed to commingle great hope with little faith; the ministers, chancellors, viziers and wizards were holding their breath. And yet the Fabulist was drawing a blank!

"May I at this point," he finally croaked, "may I now... at this juncture... perhaps... have a little more wine?" He smiled weakly.

As his glass was refilled his Manservant appeared at his side.

"Sir," whispered the Manservant. "Are you all right?"

"Do I look like I'm all right?" hissed the Fabulist, but quietly so that no one else might hear.

"No, sir; you do not."

"I am lost," said the Fabulist, and he emptied his glass in the style of the Prince, in one swallow.

"But surely this is not the time to despair!" said the Manservant. "Be bold! Strike out! Overcome!"

"Alas," said the Fabulist, "I fear I am overcome myself."

"I don't believe it, sir. You are the Fabulist!"

"Bah!"

"But sir," began the Manservant, but then he could not continue, for like the Fabulist he did not know what to say.

"Gentlemen," said the King, "are you with us?"

"In a moment," said the Manservant. "The Fabulist is... gathering his thoughts."

"My thoughts!" said the Fabulist.

"Sir!" whispered the Manservant. "Get a grip on yourself!"

"That is what I am finally doing."

"But the pillory! The yellow paint!"

"Bring them on," said the Fabulist miserably.

"Please, sir... just listen to me for a moment, for I think I see the root of the problem. There have always been men who like yourself put their faith in God, and there have always been those who like the Prince do not."

"And so there always will be. Who am I to think I can harmonize the two, or make one into the other with my puny fables?"

"But sir, not all who deny God act as the Prince does. Many are sincerely good, and treat their fellow man with kindness and respect. Isn't that so?"

The Fabulist was silent.

"Clearly they find another reason for right conduct," said the Manservant. "And now... so must you."

The Fabulist passed his hands over his face.

"Do you remember what you once said to me?" asked the Manservant. "You said, 'God shows to each man the face he is most ready to see.'"

The Fabulist looked up. "Did I say that?" he said.

"You did," lied the Manservant.

Just then the Prince rose unsteadily. "Father," he said, "now that I have slain your Goliath, may I go?"

The King sighed. "I suppose you might as well," he said. "I suppose we *all* might as well."

The Prince turned to leave. "One moment," said the Fabulist, also rising.

"Really, sir," said the King, "I think the occasion has passed."

"I couldn't agree with you more," said the

Fabulist, "and no longer will I presume to have anything to teach the Prince, or anything to teach anyone for that matter. My experiences here in Uaxala have cured me of *that*."

"Then we have done the world a service," said the Prince. "Good night."

"And yet," said the Fabulist, "I ask that you do me a last favor. Grant me one last opportunity to play the fool, for that is something I cannot give up so easily. Then you may handle me as you will," he added, looking at the King.

"Hmm..." said the King.

"Can't it wait?" said the Prince. "I have an appointment."

"At this hour?" said the King.

"Yes."

"Then you shall have to disappoint your whore."

"It's not with a whore," the Prince said, but he sat down anyway—in part because his father commanded it, and in larger part because he could not resist another opportunity to embarrass the Fabulist.

The Fabulist cleared his throat. "Thank you," he said. "I shall call this story, which is coming to me for the first time even as I speak..."

THE KING, THE TELESCOPE AND THE FACE OF GOD

A mighty King, bored by his earthly power which

extended over a vast empire and the lives and deaths of countless subjects, acquired a telescope through which one could see the face of God. It came with the following instructions:

1. Construct a tripod from the bones of long-dead hermits, monks, martyrs and saints.

("Easy enough," thought the King.)

2. Affix the telescope to the tripod and place it in the middle of a boundless desert. There build around it a labyrinth so vast that a man could wander through it for years without ever traversing the same passages or chambers twice.

("Hmm..." thought the King. "That's a little daunting, but if anyone can do it, I'm the fellow.")

3. Kill the architect who builds the labyrinth, as well as anyone else with knowledge of its plan. Burn the plan.

("I like this part! But I'll have to keep it secret from the royal architect.")

4. Enter the labyrinth, whose single entrance should be the same as its single exit, and search for the telescope. But be careful not to look through it until the night of a celestial syzygy, when the five visible planets are in perfect alignment. For if the telescope is looked through at any time other than during the syzygy, the lens will distort and show not the face of God but a vision of Hell so frightening anyone who sees it will go mad.

5. Point the telescope along the line of the syzygy, and behold — the face of God!

The King summoned the royal astronomer. "When is the next syzygy?" he asked.

The astronomer answered, "In 43 years, seven months, 21 days, twelve hours and 39 seconds, O Mighty One."

"Not much time," said the King. "We'd better get started right away!"

Soldiers were dispatched to the ends of the earth to gather the bones of long-dead hermits, monks, martyrs and saints. To do so, they had to desecrate many holy shrines and slaughter many priests and defenders of many faiths, fighting many wars in consequence. When enough bones had been gathered for 10,000 tripods, a magnificent one was constructed by the most skilled craftsmen and artisans in the kingdom. Truly it was a marvel to look upon, intricately wrought as it was, finely filigreed with zodiacal symbols, and minutely tuned and calibrated. The telescope was affixed to it, and carried to the center of the great southern desert, where work was begun immediately to build the labyrinth around it.

This was a colossal undertaking. It required the felling of entire forests that had stood since the beginning of time, and the quarrying to rubble of entire mountain ranges. For decades every inhabitant of the Kingdom was occupied exclusively in building the labyrinth—even the women, who wove tapestries and rugs for its endless walls and floors, and even the children, who were set to menial tasks such as carrying away debris and gong farming. A vast city sprang up at the edge of the labyrinth site, which itself was so large it dwarfed this city and all others in the kingdom, including the capital. Messengers arrived in the capital every hour with reports on the labyrinth's progress, monitored closely by the King. The syzygy was fast approaching, and if the labyrinth was not completed soon, there wouldn't be enough time for the King's slaves to find in advance the way to the chamber with the telescope (being careful, of course, not to look through the telescope, lest they be driven mad by a vision of Hell).

The King, who had not been young when he had acquired the telescope, was now quite old and enfeebled. No one knew whether he would live long enough to see the labyrinth completed, let alone to see the face of God. What was worse, his eyesight was failing despite the efforts of the royal college of physicians, who every morning at the King's command transplanted into his head a fresh pair of eyes plucked from a newborn baby. All this only made the King more determined, and there was much whispering in the Kingdom about the vanity of a King who went to such lengths to look upon the face of God, when any day now he would be standing before Him to be judged. But of course no one dared voice these sentiments aloud, for the King's spies were everywhere. Still, risking death, some of the royal physicians formed a secret society called the Society of the Innocent, which they dedicated to the care of the unfortunate eyeless babies whom they saw as special victims of the King's *arrogance and cruelty.*

How many thousands perished in the building of the labyrinth! Their bones were crushed to powder and mixed with its mortar. How many thousands more were slain when the labyrinth was finally completed, exactly one year before the syzygy! That night, the streets of Labyrinthium, as the city outside the labyrinth's single portal had come to be called, ran red with the blood of all those who had ever seen any of architects plans, which themselves were so numerous they filled an entire library. The library was burned to the ground in a fire so bright it could be seen at night in the far-off capital by the royal architect's wife, children, grandchildren and great-grandchildren, who did not yet know it was his funeral pyre.

Thousands of slaves then streamed into the labyrinth, with instructions to find the telescope or die. The King was moved on a golden palanquin to Labyrinthium, where he anxiously awaited word of their success. Night after night he waited in vain, and his rage grew so great that he would allow no one to be in his presence. Could it be that after all the King had caused to be done, the syzygy would pass with the telescope still not found within the labyrinth? It was unthinkable! Everyone in Labyrinthium who could walk was sent into the labyrinth, and at last, as the sun was setting to begin the very night of the syzygy, the great bell at the labyrinth's single portal rang out. The telescope had been found.

The King's palanquin was rushed to the laby-

rinth. Yet once inside, the passages and chambers were so crowded with people the palanquin could barely move. "Out of the way!" shouted the Captain of the Guard. "Forward!" he cried, whipping the palanquin bearers, who in their headlong rush trampled everyone before them so that the King was literally borne along on the backs of his people. When a bearer became exhausted, or died from a burst heart, two new bearers took his place to carry the King on and on, ever deeper into the labyrinth.

It was now after midnight, but the palanquin was still many miles from the telescope. "Faster!" shouted the captain. "Faster!" And then a further difficulty arose: the royal architect had learned that he was to be killed when the labyrinth was completed, so he built along the route to its center a series of booby traps in order to avenge himself from beyond the grave. These were triggered by the planets as one by one they moved into alignment. Bottomless pits opened in the floor, and the palanquin was nearly lost; great stones fell out of the ceiling, narrowly missing the palanquin; and walls collapsed. But the palanquin raced on.

At last, just as the syzygy was about to achieve its most perfect linearity, the palanquin arrived at the labyrinth's central chamber. The Captain of the Guard lifted out the King and set him before the telescope. The King reached for it with gnarled fingers trembling from greed, and aimed it through a hole in the ceiling directly above. He put his eye to the eyepiece and there in the lens were the five visible planets, lined up in the night sky like a glowing pointer... yet beyond the last planet he saw was nothing: only stars.

"It's a cheat," said the King. "I've been cheated!"

"What is it, sire?" said the Captain of the Guard.

"There's no face of God!" screamed the King. "There's nothing!"

"Try the focus," suggested the captain, and the King twisted the knob. Suddenly the planets were blotted out, and the lens filled up with a soft white blur.

"Ah!" said the King. He focused in. Then he whispered, "No! It can't be!"

"What do you see, sire?" said the Captain of the Guard. But instead of answering, the King shrieked horribly, staggered back and fell. "Sire!" the captain shouted, and rushed to where the King lay face down. He turned the King over, and the eyes that looked up at him were empty as the void — the eyes of a hopeless madman.

"Blue," whispered the King. "No, I think green this morning — or brown? Perhaps grey!"

The captain let the King's head drop. So, he thought, smiling grimly, they were too late after all. The syzygy had ended and the King had been driven mad by a vision of hell. The captain turned and looked at the telescope. Was there anything he could see through it that would be worse than the countless battlefields on which he'd stood in waist-deep gore, cutting men to pieces even as he looked forward to raping and cutting to pieces their wives and daughters, and slaughtering their sons as well? And should Hell be worse, wasn't that more reason to look now, since no doubt he would find himself there when his time came? At least he would know what to expect. He rose and peered through the telescope. But to his surprise, the planets were still in alignment; the syzygy was not over after all. Yet he saw no vision of Hell; neither did he see the face of God. He saw only stars.

Meanwhile, on the roof of the labyrinth directly above the chamber, two physicians from the Society of the Innocent were gazing down through the hole that had been cut for the telescope.

"He might see you," whispered one of the physicians.

"Don't worry," said the other. "It's over." He was holding the newborn baby whose eyes had been plucked from their sockets that very morning and transplanted into the King. Tenderly, he pulled the blankets closer about the baby, for a cool wind had begun to blow in this hour before dawn.

"You did well, little one," he said, and softly kissed the eyeless baby's cheek. "Now let's go home."

"I pronounce no official moral on this fable," concluded the Fabulist, "but leave each of you to draw your own." He sat down to silence, which he took as a sign that his story had beglamoured the Uaxalans completely. His Manservant too seemed awed into silence... so why did he look so frightened? Shouldn't he have been pleased and proud? In fact, now that the Fabulist looked around at the company, it seemed they were not enchanted by his story at all; they were mortified! They were avoiding his eyes, or whispering to one another while glancing at him, or exchanging worried glances amongst themselves. And the King? His hands were covering his face. But the Prince! He jumped up shouting "Bravo!"

The Fabulist stared at him in surprise.

"Bravo!" repeated the Prince. "I take back all those bad things I said about you... I am ashamed of them, I regret them, they were false and undeserved! You are a great philosopher—a genius!"

"You... you liked my story?" asked the Fabulist.

"I loved it!" said the Prince. "It was brilliant!"

"You don't want to change the ending?"

"Change it? Not a word!"

"Or continue it?"

"Of course not! It's perfect as it is: the revenge of the innocent upon the vain and cruel!"

"Well yes, but—"

"Thank you," said the Prince. "Your story means more to me than you know." He turned to the King. "Thank you too, father, for this evening—for bringing this man here. I shall never forget him or his wonderful tale... and neither, I think, shall you."

"Hal," said the King in a stricken voice.

"I must go," said the Prince. He began to back away. "Really I must! Don't beg me to stay! I'm late!" And he turned and ran toward the doors of the hall.

"Hal!" his father cried after him. "Hal, please, come back! Son!" But the Prince called back only "Farewell!" and was gone.

Meanwhile the Fabulist had whispered to his Manservant, "What is wrong?"

"Don't you see, sir?" said the Manservant.

"No I don't! What have I done?"

"You told a tale of revenge!"

"In a sense. But the *real* meaning—"

"Fool!" shouted the King at the Fabulist. "Dunce! Dunderhead! Ignoramus!"

"But Your Majesty," began the Fabulist.

"Shut up!" roared the King.

"But—"

"*Shut up!* Haven't you done enough with your endlessly flapping mouth? Haven't you any sense at all?"

"Show me where I have erred," begged the Fabulist. "Please! I don't understand!"

"How could you tell the Prince such a story? In which the principal theme is revenge?"

"That is the *ostensible* theme, I agree. But the *principal* theme is compassion for our fellow men!"

"Rubbish!" said the King.

"But the Society of the Innocent weren't seeking revenge! They simply wished to prevent further cruelty! And this they accomplished not by appealing to God for miracles or moral authority, which the Prince would disdain as you know, but simply by making the King—who, by the way, in no way is meant to suggest yourself, Your Majesty—they simply forced him to see the suffering he had caused!"

"That may be as you say," said the King, "yet it was lost on the Prince. Didn't you hear him? He said 'revenge of the innocent upon the vain and cruel!'"

"But give him time, Your Majesty. The Prince is thoughtful by nature, and I am certain he will dig beneath the story's surface."

"Had your story ended otherwise, I might agree with you," said the King. "But the Prince is so fixated upon his own suffering and that of his poor dead mother, and he so uncontrollably hates those who caused it… no, what you have done is inexcusable. Did you not know the circumstances of his mother's death?"

"I did," said the Fabulist. "My Manservant discovered it from one of your servants."

"He 'discovered' nothing," sneered the King. "We instructed that good woman to tell him, knowing he would tell you."

"But why didn't you just tell me directly?"

cried the Fabulist.

"We could not! The Prince would have flown into a rage had he learned of it, so touchy is he upon this subject. We had to communicate it to you indirectly, and hope you would twig its significance. Vain hope! Misplaced confidence! You, of all men—have sensitivity!"

The Fabulist hung his head.

"No," said the King, "you were too taken with your creation to sense its inappropriateness, too in love with your tale as you were spinning it, too... *too everything you ought not to have been!*"

"I was," sobbed the Fabulist.

"Captain!" shouted the King, and his Captain of the Guard sprang forward. "Take this... this *regrettable* man to the tower. And his Manservant, too, because that's how angry I am!"

The Fabulist said not a word as the captain led him from the hall, but shuffled along despondently head down. The Uaxalan nobility were silent as well, for now that they saw how utterly crushed the Fabulist was, they were ashamed of their earlier eagerness for it— especially since many found the Fabulist's story quite artful.

The Manservant however did not go quietly. "Your Majesty!" he cried as the guards dragged him out. "It's not his fault; it's mine! I led him to think of that story!" He was pulled through the doors but his head popped back in. "Please! He meant no harm! Don't hang him!" The guards carried him off down the corridor, and still his pleading could be heard. "Punish me instead, and send him home! But not in a pillory! All right—a pillory-but don't paint him! Besides, I think he has a point about his story! Wait! Wait...!"

When at last his voice had died out, the King turned to his ministers, chancellors, viziers and wizards. "We must find the Prince and determine what damage has been done," he said, "and whether it can be undone before he is provoked by this story into some rash new misbehavior. I did not like the sound of that 'Farewell!'" But though they searched all the rest of that night, and all the next day and the next night, too, visiting every disreputable den in the city and turning out the beds of every serving girl in the palace and on many of the outlying estates, the Prince could not be found.

Chapter Three: On Ship and Island

Upon leaving the feast after the Fabulist's story, the Prince hurried by dark alleys and hidden byways to the docks, where a longboat awaited him. The hired oarsman rowed out of the harbor and asked, "Where exactly are we going, Your Highness?"

"Round that far point," said the Prince. "There should be a signal."

"A signal?" asked the man.

"A light."

"Ashore?"

"On a ship."

"Oh, I don't like it, Your Majesty; I don't mind saying so at all. What sort of ship with what sort of crew would be hiding round the point in the darkness, making secret signals and such?"

The Prince did not want to say, "It's the *Bloody Doodle-Doo*, of course, crewed by forty murderous and implacable pirates and commanded by the infamous Slag himself, who was not beheaded by the Mamelukes, as everyone

says, but is very much in possession of his head."
Nor did he wish to explain that he, the Prince,
had promised to lead these pirates to the secret
island where they might, at their leisure, violate,
torture and kill or capture (to use and sell as
slaves) thousands of unprotected women (his
father's wives) and even more young girls (their
daughters, his own half-sisters). So he merely
said, "That's my affair, not yours."

"Oh, I ought to be home in bed with my
Poll," said the man. "That's where *I* ought to be.
Sure she's ugly, and a fishwife, I'll admit, but—"

"More rowing-less talking!" cried the Prince,
who could scarcely contain his impatience. At
last he was embarked upon the grim work he had
awaited so long! At last the wicked wives and
deceitful daughters would be repaid like for like
for the evil they had done, for the meaningless
death they had inflicted (as a trick!) upon his
mother, and for the pain and emptiness and
dreadful horror in remembering it that weighed
him down every moment of every day, even
when he sought to lose himself in the physical act
of love, and even when he slept, for when he
awoke each morning (or afternoon, as was the
case) his pillow was soaked with tears. Nay, they
would be repaid ten times over, and this was as it
should be, since they were vain and cruel and
deserved what they were about to get, while his
mother had been innocent and undeserving of

her suffering. Yet despite the truth of all this—
despite his magnificent, unprecedented hatred—
as the night of rendezvous with the pirates had
drawn near, he had found himself growing un-
easy. It was not that he, too, would be murdered
by the pirates (most likely), or at the very least
never see Uaxala again. No, he had long ago
made friends with the prospect of death or lonely
self-exile. He embraced it as he would embrace
oblivion. Rather he was troubled (and was troubled that he was troubled) by the loathsomeness
of what would happen on the island. Why, earlier
this evening he had almost suffered a complete
failure of nerve, and resolved not to keep his
rendezvous after all! And then the Fabulist had
told that wonderful story—and all of the Prince's
doubts, qualms, equivocations, misgivings, second thoughts, and cowardly reluctances had
been swept away. For the story clearly legiti-
mized all he was about to set in motion, in both
human and divine terms—human because a non-
believer such as himself could say that men alone
had been the agents of retribution in the story,
and divine because a believer such as the Fabulist, or his father, could say that God had chosen
to act through men. It could not have been more
perfect had the Fabulist actually known what the
Prince was up to! (Had he? No; that was impossible... the Prince was certain he'd never let it slip
to anyone, no matter how drunk he'd been in a

tavern or how unguarded in a woman's arms.) Somehow, by instinct or fate or plain dumb luck, the Fabulist had hit the nail on the head, and the Prince almost wished the Fabulist were there in the boat with him now, so that the Prince might kiss him in gratitude.

At length a light was spotted. But as they drew near, the oarsman stopped rowing.

"Your Majesty... what ship is that?" he asked.

"The ship where you shall leave me," said the Prince.

The oarsman narrowed his eyes at it, and then his mouth dropped open. "She's got black sails!" he gasped. "And she's flying the Jolly Roger!"

"You're mistaken," said the Prince.

"I ain't mistaken either! I know that ship! It's the *Bloody Doodle-Doo!*"

"Keep your voice down," said the Prince.

But the man began to tremble. "Let's get away afore they see us!" he said. "Hush now! I'm turning!"

"You'll take me to the ship," said the Prince. "That is what I have paid you to do."

"Aye," said the man, "but you ain't paid me to get my throat cut!"

"They won't harm you. I won't let them."

"No sir!"

"I give you my word as your Prince, you

fool!"

"I don't mean no disrespect, Your Worship… only your word means one thing to you, and another thing entirely to them!"

"Then get out," said the Prince. "Swim back. I shall row myself." But at that moment a hand sprang up from the water to the gunwale, and a cutlass flashed up in another hand, and like that the oarsman was run through. "Poll!" he croaked weakly as his last breath rattled out of him.

"Murderer!" cried the Prince, standing up, for a pirate was pulling himself into the boat. "Why did you do that?"

"Captain's orders," said the pirate, who was stripped to the waist and covered with tattoos. He rolled the dead man into the water. "The Captain's a cautious one, he is," he said, and settled in at the oars. Then he looked up at the Prince. "Sit down, Your Royal Loveliness—if you please, that is. Yer rocking the boat."

Soon the Prince found himself on the deck of the *Bloody Doodle-Doo*, standing before Captain Slag, whom the Prince had not met before, having communicated with him through unseen intermediaries who never stepped out of the shadows. Now, this Slag was seven feet tall, and his bare tattooed chest was so broad and mighty he almost couldn't see the Prince over it. As Slag bent down slightly to peer at the Prince, the Prince started back even though (like every Uaxalan child) he'd heard tales of the captain's astonishing appearance. For his eyeballs glowed yellow and never stood still in their sockets, but jumped and goggled and revolved in opposing directions, one west to east as the earth revolves, and the other east to west like the transit of the sun. To be stared at by those eyes was dizzying, especially in the flickering lantern-light aboard the ship, yet the Prince could not have said whether they were the most unnerving thing about the captain's face. That might have been his enormous nose, which was swollen from rum and covered with warts, wens, scabs, pustules, boils, hives, blackheads, cysts, rashes, hairy carbuncles, fistulas, polyps, blisters and poxes, all piled and encrusted on top of one another... or it might have been his cheeks, which were pierced from the inside by sharks' teeth and dragons' claws, so that his cheeks looked like a spiked ball... or it might have been that mouth, which was a long deep gash like a knife wound, from which his putrid breath poured forth like black smoke. As for clothes, on his head the Captain wore a woman's purple hat with a broad floppy brim and tall purple plumes, and about his groin a foul stinking diaper that did little to conceal his mighty package. And that was all he wore, tattoos of black gunpowder serving instead to clothe his body, which was humped all over with weird knots, muscles and sinews.

"I am Slag," said the captain in an odd harsh whisper that came from having his voice box crushed by a hangman's rope, from which he'd swung for eight days and nights without strangling before being rescued by his men. (His neck also bore chop marks like the bole of an ancient oak too strong for the ax, from the Mamelukes having tried but failed to cut off his head.) "Once I was set upon by a thousand Cyclops," he said, "and having no weapons to hand, I shat upon the ground a giant turd which I hardened to stone with my fiery breath, and wielding it as a truncheon did cave in all their skulls."

"Aye, he made porridge of their brains and porridge bowls of their brain pans!" cried the pirates, who were crowded around at the edge of the light. "We saw it all!"

"Once," continued Slag, "I did battle with a thousand man-killing Amazons, whereupon I cast my weapons away in contempt and did forcibly pleasure them to death."

"Aye, they lay smoking from the loins!" cried the pirates. "We saw it all!"

"To make widows of wives, orphans of children, corpses of both and meals out of corpses— too sweet to me is that. Sweet also is the making of villages into firepits, towns into charnel houses, and entire great cities into ash heaps. You see," he said, the ends of his mouth curving downwards, for that was how he smiled, "I like to make things!"

The pirates roared delightedly. "He likes to *make* things!" they cackled. "*Make* things! Great Slag!" Then one by one they fell silent and looked at the Prince, for now it was his turn to speak.

"I am Prince Hal," he began, but like the Fabulist earlier that evening, for the first time ever he did not know what to say. For the first time since he'd been paralyzed by Undine's potion, he felt like a scared helpless child. Yet he could not let the pirates see this... was he not, after all, the Prince? "At one, I could spell 'incorrigible,'" he said. "At two, I beat the King at chess, and at three, I foretold an earthquake."

Slag laughed, a great rumbling laugh so much like thunder that lightning seemed to shoot out of his eyes. The pirates laughed too, in their own fiendish ways, shrieking and cackling and splitting their sides. When this had subsided, Slag fixed one eye on the Prince while the other eye spun slowly backwards. "So here you are at last, my lassie" he said. "These pretty lassies," and here he indicated his crew who were all men as far as the Prince could see, "were afraid you'd changed your mind and weren't coming."

"I... I had to stop at a feast at the palace," said the Prince.

"A feast! How sweet for you! And were there lots of pretty lassies there like yourself?"

"I'd prefer that you didn't call me a lass,"

said the Prince. The pirates tittered and slavered.

"Very well then, my lassie," said Slag. "What would you like me to call you?"

"Hal would be fine."

"Fair enough, pretty Hal."

"I'd prefer also—that is, I wish you hadn't—I mean you oughtn't to have killed the man who rowed my boat."

Slag laughed again, this time like an exploding volcano. Then he held forth his huge hand, his eyes revolving faster, and he hissed, "Give us the chart. We're anxious to be under way."

The Prince was silent.

"You do have the chart... don't you?"

"No," said the Prince. "I burned it." At this, the pirates growled and gnashed their teeth, and pressed in menacingly with drawn swords.

"But not," continued the Prince, "before committing it to memory."

"Argh," growled the captain. "You'd better hope your memory is a good one, then." But his face softened, or so it seemed to the Prince, although he could not be sure. "I mean, only if you want your proper vengeance, that is," Slag said.

"I do," said the Prince.

"Then give us a heading."

"South and westward, 76 degrees for 12 leagues due—"

"We don't hold with such science," said Captain Slag sourly.

The Prince pointed at the horizon. "Sail toward that star," he said.

The pirates jumped and whooped and disappeared up the rigging into darkness as Slag exhorted them hoarsely, "Sheet home, ye dried up streaks of piss! Trice up! Lay out! The more canvas we fly the sooner you'll reach your heart's delight!"

"How far be it, Cap'n?" called one of the men from above.

Slag's restless eyes rotated round at the Prince. "Three weeks by the chart," the Prince said.

"Aye, but that's for lesser ships," said Slag, "not for the *Bloody Doodle-Doo*. Grind your cutlasses and peel back your ragged foreskins!" he cried to his crew. "Before sunup tomorrow, we'll be splitting open fair damsels with both!"

"Metal and meat!" roared the crew in the rigging. "Metal and meat for the pretties!"

Hours later, the Prince had climbed into the crow's-nest, as the crew of the *Bloody Doodle-Doo* were so evil-smelling he had been desperate for air. Pirates were still scampering about on the ropes and spars, putting out the last sails (for the ship was flying them all, from the catch-if-you-can before the jibs, to the main topgallant staysail, to the spanker stretched out astern), but even so, they were far below the Prince's aerie. He could hear them calling instructions to one another in the darkness—"Stand to! Haul on! Knot it back!"—and there also came drifting up to him whispered intimacies that turned his stomach, such as "Kiss me, lover," and "Ooh, yer warm as a roasted chestnut!" The pirates were better than he hoped for, yet also worse than he feared. The "better" part was this: the pirates' startling blood-thirstiness and depravity guaranteed that his enemies would suffer as much as he thought they ought to. Yet this was also the "worse" part, for his pangs of conscience had returned! He did not believe in Heaven or Hell or spirits or even souls, but he whispered, "Mother, make me strong enough to do what must be done." And just as the King in the Fabulist's story had sought the face of God in the stars, so the Prince sought his mother's face among the constellations of the Uaxalan winter sky. There were Cetus the Sea Monster, the Triangulum Australe, and Mensa the Table Mountain, near his favorite: Horologium the Clock. They swayed above him, antipodal to the swaying of the crow's-nest. And between the swaying and his exhaustion and the great quantities of wine he had drunk, the Prince fell asleep.

He dreamed he was already on the island. It was night; at his feet a giant figure lay writhing upon the ground: Slag, face down, thrusting downward with his mighty hips. Beneath him, bearing the force of this, was Undine, who ought to have been obscured by Slag's bulk, but thanks to the curious laws of dreams, the Prince could see her perfectly well.

"Help me," Undine whimpered. "Help me—in the name of God!"

"Yes," said Slag between grunts. "Help her."

The Prince knelt beside her. A gleaming dagger was in his hand, and he drew it slowly across Undine's throat so that her warm blood spurted out upon Slag. "He slit her like a haggis!" cried the voices of the pirates out of the darkness. "We saw it all!" The Prince shrank back, horrified by what he had done, yet exultant at the same time. He turned and saw that he was on a great field of slaughter, under a blood red sky. The King's wives and their daughters lay strewn about, and the pirates moved among them like reapers, swinging their blades in long measured strokes and bending now and then to ravish or excruciate. As they sowed they sang a song that rang out above the screams of the women:

> *Chop, chop, chop!*
> *Slice, slice, slice!*
> *Killing missies sure be nice!*
> *Swive 'em first or*
> *Swive 'em during,*
> *Either way be real alluring!*

The Prince stood before an open black door-way.

"Go in," Slag whispered in his ear. "She's waiting for you."

"Who?" said the Prince, not taking his eyes from the doorway.

"The last one! The lads had some fun with her, but we saved her for you!"

The Prince moved toward the doorway. As he passed through into darkness he heard Slag hiss behind him, "Finish it!"

The Prince was in a labyrinth. At times, it was the labyrinth in the palace garden, in which he and his mother had played so happily, though he had not set foot in it since her death; and at times it was the vast labyrinth from the Fabulist's story. He rushed through it with ever-growing urgency, for the "last one" who he must find seemed always to be just around the next corner or in the next chamber or passage, yet always she eluded him. A year passed, and then another, and still the Prince searched the empty labyrinth. Suddenly, he came upon the dead oarsman, who stood dripping wet from the sea, with seaweed in his hair and fishtails sticking out of his pockets. Wordlessly he raised an arm and pointed to the labyrinth's central chamber. The Prince entered, but in the gloom could see nothing, apart from a heap of rags in the corner. Where could she be? Why had the oarsman sent him in here? Then the rags moved… she *was* there, the last one, hiding beneath them! The dagger was once more in his hand, and though he did not grip it with his fingers it seemed stuck to his palm of its own accord. He advanced upon the rags… and then he heard his mother calling distantly, just as she had called when he lay paralyzed in the labyrinth in the garden.

"Hal!" his mother called over and over, drawing closer. "Hal, come out, come out!"

"Here!" he cried, greatly relieved not to be paralyzed this time. "Mother! Here I am!" He ran to the doorway… and there she was: his mother! How he loved her! How he missed her! On her face there was a look of great concern and urgency.

"Hal," she said, "Oh Hal!"

"Mother!"

"But what are you doing?"

"Avenging you! At last they will pay for what they did to you—for what they did to both of us!"

"Oh Hal!" she cried, and came towards him. But as he held out his arms to receive her, she rushed past as if he were not there. She hurried to the corner, where she lifted the heap of rags to her breast. "Dear God!" she cried, looking down into the rags and shedding great tears. "What have you done?" Now she raised her face and screamed at the Prince, *"What have you done?"* The rags fell away, and the Prince saw that she held a baby whose eyes had been plucked from their sockets.

The Prince awoke greatly shaken. It was dawn, and the *Bloody Doodle-Doo* plunged on. "I've been a fool!" he wailed, smiting himself on the head and breast. "A fool, a fool—a damned evil-doer as bad as God Himself!" He pulled his hair and bit his fingers, and nearly threw himself out of the crow's-nest to the waves below. What stopped him was this: he would then be a coward as well as an evil-doer. No; he could not die with all those deaths on his conscience—or, if he had to die that way, at least let it be bravely, trying to prevent them. He would try to divert the pirates from the island. But how? Any moment now they would sight it, and perhaps they would kill him right then. He would fight them; he would kill as many as he could, which might be more than a few, as he was fairly nimble with a sword... but in the end, the King's wives and their daughters would die just the same. If only there were a way to turn the pirates, or trick them, or....

The Prince knew what he must do. He must challenge Slag to fight to the death, and he must not allow himself to be killed, but must kill the man who could not be hung or decapitated or overwhelmed by a thousand Cyclops. Then by pirate law, he, the Prince, would be captain of the *Bloody Doodle-Doo*, and the crew would be obliged to do as he said.

Now if only he knew how Slag might be killed!

"Oh, well," he shrugged. "I'm sure I'll think of something." And he descended from the crow's-nest to the deck.

Slag stood alone upon the poop royal, searching the horizon with a spyglass made from white bones.

"Captain Slag!" the Prince called up to him, approaching.

"Don't see the island yet, my pretty lassie," said Slag, not lowering the spyglass. "But they're close—I can smell 'em!"

The Prince thought it best to dive right in. "Captain," he said, "I'm sorry to have inconvenienced you, but I've changed my mind."

Slag did not hear. "*Chop chop chop, slice slice slice,*" he sang to himself.

"Captain Slag," repeated the Prince, "I said I've changed my mind and would like to turn back now."

Still, Slag seemed not to hear. But some of the pirates had, and they drew near to see what it was about. The Prince eyed them warily but persisted.

"Captain," he said, "excuse me. There is something we must talk about."

At last, Slag dropped the glass from his eye

and turned to look down at the Prince. In anticipation of this day Slag had rouged his cheeks so that the sharks' teeth and dragons' claws poking through them had clots of red powder and shreds of powder-puff at their points; as he had no lips to speak of, he had outlined his gash-like mouth with red greasepaint; and his eyes now spun in a band of purple, which matched his hat but made him look like a purple raccoon. "Ain't I pretty?" he hissed.

"Yes, quite lovely," said the Prince. "But I'm afraid you've troubled yourself for nothing."

"I don't get ye," said Slag.

"I am no longer interested in revenge. I want everyone on that island left in peace, and I wish to be returned to Uaxala forthwith."

Slag grinned his upside-down grin. "No," he said simply.

"I insist upon it," said the Prince.

"He *insists* upon it!" roared Slag, and the pirates who had gathered round echoed, "He insists! The Prince insists!"

"I do," said Hal.

"Kill him," Slag said mildly to his crew.

"Me!" shouted a Fiji islander who sprang forward twirling razors above his head. "I will carve him with my singing twin blades!"

"No, me!" shouted another pirate, holding up a hook where his hand should have been. "I will gut him with me hungry crampon!"

"Stand back," shouted a third, stepping out of his pants. "I will tear him from behind with my double-headed thruster!"

"Stop!" said the Prince. "I challenge Slag."

The pirates stared for a moment in astonishment, then fell laughing about the deck.

"*You?*" said Slag. "Challenge *me*?"

The Prince nodded.

Slag threw back his head and laughed with the sound of a thundering herd of wooly mammoths. The mizzen mainsail above him blew outward from his laughter, its stays and braces snapping musically like guitar-strings. He leapt down to the deck, which boomed and heaved from the impact, and stood before the Prince. "Gaze ye upon my tattoos," he said. "Here on my belly is the poor fool who dueled me with cannon. Being a fair man I let him fire first. I caught his cannonball in my teeth and spat it back with such force, it tore off his head."

"Aye, Slag never even touched his own cannon!" cried the pirates. "We saw it all!"

"And here," continued Slag, "is the doomed creature who jousted me with harpoons, using whales as our mounts. With one mighty stroke I slew him and his whale, and my own whale as well for good measure."

"Aye, Slag cut a gully in the sea with that stroke! We saw it all!"

"Beneath this is depicted the cannibal king

who did engage me with living bludgeons."

"Living bludgeons?" said the Prince.

"Aye," said Slag. "We swung slaves by the ankles with which to batter one another. His slave broke apart on my chest, and I bashed him so titanically the bodies fused together into one corpse with two heads."

This story seemed to be a favorite of the crew, for they had no comment upon it but howled with great merriment.

"Now," said Slag, leaning his awful face into the Prince's, "how do *you* wish to duel me?"

The Prince reeled back from Slag's smoke-like breath. What weapon could he choose that might give him some slim chance for survival? Perhaps he ought to go with the epée or the stinger, which depended upon quickness and agility instead of strength. But what use would such delicate weapons be against Slag? His belly was covered with tattoos of men who had fought him with all manner of swords and firearms, and all had gone down to dusty or watery death. There were so many of these tattoos that soon Slag's belly, and much of the rest of him, would be rendered solid black.

"Hmm," thought the Prince. "His tattoos...!" And just as he had assumed upon descending from the crow's-nest, a method for killing Slag did in fact come to him. If you have been paying proper attention to the detailed description of

Slag's person (missing not a word, for all are important), you may have an inkling of this method, in which case you will be very sorry not to be able to warn the Prince to give up the idea, as it will seem unlikely in conception, unworkable in execution, and destined to disaster. But if you do not yet have such an inkling, do not worry; you will have plenty of fun watching it play out.

"Well, then," said Slag. "What'll it be?"

"I may fight you with anything?" asked the Prince.

"Anything," said Slag. "The more novel the better, for killing people in ordinary ways has long ago grown tiresome for me."

"Very well," said the Prince. "I choose to fight you with a nail and a match."

Slag laughed like an earthquake that shakes the sea floor and raises towering waves to crash down on ships. His crew brayed like asses and wiped their grimy eyes with grimy fingers. "A *nail*, did you say? And a *match*? Does it have to be a *big* nail?" Slag mocked. "Or will a small one kill me just as well?"

"A small one is sufficient, as long as it is stout," said the Prince. "And the match must have plenty of sulfur."

A leering pirate appeared instantly with two nails and two matches. "Thank you," said the Prince, taking one of each. But when the fellow approached, he was toppled him onto his head with a clout. "Get away with that!" growled Slag.

By now all the pirates had gathered round in a circle, and the bloodlust in their eyes was frightening. "Make it last," they begged Slag. "Don't kill him straight off!" Slag chuckled as an indulgent father chuckles. He set his hands on his hips, threw out his chest, which the Prince did not think could be thrown out any further, and said, "Do your worst, Your Highness."

Now it would not be accurate to say the Prince was scared, for he wasn't—not as you or I would be, because he was a Prince, and we are not. But neither would it be accurate to say he was *not* scared, for he was a thinking person as well as a Prince. Say therefore that he was daunted by the odds against him, yet determined to triumph over them anyhow; that he expected to die, yet hoped to take his foe with him; that he was, in a word, *resolute*. He tucked the match in his waistband for later use, and holding the nail before him circled cautiously, as he'd been taught by his fencing instructor. Slag and the pirates thought this such a funny sight that they nearly bepissed themselves with laughter. The Prince seized this as his opportunity, and he leapt upon Slag's chest and began poking him repeatedly with the nail—not deeply, but just enough to make little holes in the skin. At this Slag laughed harder, for he was truly enjoying the Prince's antics, and the Prince went to work on his belly. He made dozens of holes before Slag became irritated and swatted him off. The Prince flew into the air from the force of this swat, and would have continued flying far out to sea if he had not been caught by the fore-topgallant studding sail, from which he slid into the fore-topgallant stay-sail, from which he slid into the fore-topmast studding sail and then into the fore-topmast staysail, and so on from sail to sail until he slipped from the lowest and thudded onto the deck below. He was dragged to his feet by the pirates, yet when he tried to stand he cried out and fell, for his right leg was broken. He was dragged to his feet again, or rather to his one good foot, and flamingo-like he watched Slag striding towards him from the stern—watched him with his one good eye, that is, for the other was swollen shut. Also, his mouth was full of sharp stones which he realized were teeth, and these he spat out with much blood.

"Need this?" asked Slag, holding up the Prince's nail between his thumb and forefinger.

"No, thank you," lisped the Prince. "I am finithed with it."

Slag crushed it to dust and blew the dust away. The Prince realized he had arrived at the critical moment of his plan, for in leaping upon Slag with the nail he had been aided by the surprising nature and ridiculousness of his attack—a tactic that would not work twice. He would have to think of another way to get close to Slag.

"Captain Slag," he said (still lisping, although I will not annoy your eye by replacing every *s* with a *th*), "I see now my folly in thinking I might prevail against you. I am not afraid to die, but it grieves me that my father does not know where I am and will not know what has become of me. He will worry and wonder about me till the end of his days, which will be sooner rather than later because of this."

"Ah!" said Slag. "Too sweet to me is that!"

"Exactly," said the Prince. "In fact, no one but you pirates will know my fate. What will you do with me after I'm dead?"

"We'll eat you, of course," said Slag with his downside-up grimace, "and pick our teeth with your bones before casting them into the sea."

"Am I right in assuming I will be immortalized upon your belly?"

"Aye."

"There's some comfort in that, at least," said the Prince. "Since your belly will be my final resting place, as it were, may I take one last look at it?"

"Look away," said Slag, greatly flattered, and he rolled forth his belly as a boulder rolls out of a cave. The Prince hopped forward and scrutinized the tattoos closely. "Excellent work," he murmured. "Quite artistic." He took the match out of his waistband and held it up. "With one eye swollen shut, I am having some trouble seeing. Do you mind if I light this?"

"Arrgh," said Slag, which the Prince took as signifying indulgence. He struck the match on Slag's coarse skin, and as he continued to pour over the tattoos, he gently touched the match to each of the holes he had made with the nail.

"Mind yer match, there," said Slag.

"I'm very sorry," said the Prince. "I shall extinguish it." And he thrust the match into the hole just above Slag's belly-button, where the tattoos were the thickest. Slag started back, not in pain for he was impervious to it, but in surprise at this grave affront to his person. He brushed away the match and looked with rage upon the Prince. His eyeballs spun so fast in their sockets they whined and shot sparks, and his face became indigo and burning hot. Rearing up to a great height and raising his great balled fist above his head, he roared "Prepare to die!" And the Prince hunkered down for his last moment on earth. He would have preferred to live long enough to see whether his idea had worked, but it seemed as though he would just have to trust in it. He closed his eyes. Then Slag dashed the poor Prince upon the head so mightily that if the decking on which he stood had not been rotten and given way, absorbing much of the force of the blow, his head would have been driven down into the region of his stomach. As it was, he found himself with only his head protruding above the deck, while the rest of him dangled down into the compartment below.

"Lookee!" said Slag, pointing at the Prince's head. "A ball to kick!" The pirates hooted and guffawed, and Slag drew back his foot.

"I die happy," said the Prince, "for you are already a dead man."

Slag and the pirates laughed. "I?" Slag said, waving away a bit of smoke that had appeared from nowhere. "A dead man? I think you are confused!"

"I have killed you," said the Prince. "Look at your belly." Slag gazed upon it, as did his crew, and what they saw was this: little trails of smoke drifting upward from the many holes the Prince had poked and lighted. This was accompanied by sizzling and fizzling and popping noises, such as fuses make, for Slag's tattoos, which were etched with black gunpowder—as are all sailors' tattoos—were igniting beneath his skin.

"I'm afire on the inside!" cried Slag, and he began beating his belly with his flat, open palms. The pirates ran around in great confusion, some fetching buckets with which to fetch seawater, some rushing up to urinate upon Slag, as they felt there was no time for buckets, and others just flying about to no purpose. But it was all in vain, for no matter how much and with what they doused him, no matter how they rolled him on the deck and threw themselves on him to smother the fires, a subcutaneous red glow spread inexorably from Slag's belly to his chest and around to his back, and surged down his legs and along his arms. Smoke now poured from Slag's mouth and nostrils and ears, and his crew began to cry, "Jump! Jump overboard! Jump now!" Slag ran for the rail, but before he could reach it he exploded like a bomb with a wet *ker-flump!* Pirates, deck, masts, spars, sails, rails, rigging and so on—all were sprayed with Slag's fluids and shredded meat and bone (although the Prince was protected by a pirate who fell down dead in front of him, pierced through by flying splinters). Slag's head was blown straight up into the air. High above the crow's-nest it flew, tumbling end over end against the vault of the sky and hanging there a moment at its apogee... then down and down it plunged, landing upright on the deck with a splat, inches from the Prince's head. The Prince watched in horror as Slag's eyes opened one last time. Only now they were not revolving, but remained still as normal eyes do.

"Peace at last!" Slag rasped... and then his eyes closed forever.

Many of the crew had been killed by the explosion. Those who survived picked themselves up and gazed about in shock and disbelief. As if they were dreamers they crept between the bodies toward where Slag's head faced the Prince's on the deck.

"Slag be dead!" one whispered. It was the Fiji Islander who had twirled twin razors.

"He killed Slag!" said another, this being the fellow with the hook, or crampon as he called it.

"The Cap'n—killed by this boy!" sniffed a third, the prodigy of nature who was double-headed down below.

"I am your captain now," said the Prince as authoritatively as he could under the circumstances, for he knew his fight was not yet over. "Get me out of this hole."

The three pirates exchanged sly looks. "It do be the pirate law," Razors said.

"Aye," said Crampon, "but he aren't one of us."

"No he aren't," said Double-Headed Thruster, "so the law don't apply."

"Have I not joined you?" asked the Prince. "Have I not proved myself by killing your captain?"

"Hmm," said Razors and Crampon together, stroking their stubbly chins.

"Aye, but if he *is* our captain by reason of what he did to poor Slag," said Double-Headed, thinking aloud, "don't it follow that *I* would be captain were I to kill *him*?"

"Hmm," said Razors and Crampon again.

"If Slag could not kill me," said the Prince,

"what makes you think you can?"

"Why, yer nothing but a head in a hole," said Double-Headed. "I shall kill ye quite easily!"

"No," cried Razors, "for *I'm* a-going to do it!"

"No," cried Crampon, "for I am!" And they squared off scowling and growling at one another, razors twirling, crampon twisting hungrily, and anatomical wonder (fortunately for our sensibilities) staying where it belonged, as its owner had drawn his cutlasses instead. Thus with steely eye did the pirates eye one another, and circle round the Prince's head as around a campfire or totem.

"Stop!" said the Prince. "I, your captain, command you!" But the pirates ignored him.

"Thou gorbellied crutch!" muttered Double-Headed to either of his adversaries (it did not seem to matter which).

"Thou sassy clotpole!" countered Razors.

"Thou weather-bitten dog-borne minimus!" topped Crampon.

"Idiots!" cried the Prince, trying desperately to pull his head below deck, out of danger. But he was stuck.

Now, the other pirates who had survived the explosion of Slag were watching this, and each of them wished to be captain as well. So one by one they joined the original three, announcing themselves with fearsome curses such as, "Fen-sucked pumpion!" or "Fitful malkin!" or "Vain, puking measle, I defy you!" Round and round they went around the Prince's head, rattling their weapons, their fury mounting inexorably, while the Prince seemed to have been forgotten completely. Oaths and curses flew thickly back and forth, and now and then a pirate feinted at his neighbor or even drew a little of his own blood as a kind of warming up, as a foretaste of the gathering cataclysm. Terrible it would be when it came, and the Prince could only hope he would not be trampled to death.

Then suddenly one of the pirates cried out, "Land Ho!" But the rest would not take their eyes off one another.

"Shame on ye!" someone said. "That's a child's trick!"

"No!" said the first. "Look! 'Tis the island!"

They did look, but without breaking the circle. "Arrgh," they intoned, which the Prince took to signify their wonder and acknowledgment.

"'Tis not the island!" cried the Prince (although it was). "'Tis another we must change our course at for the real one!"

The pirates looked at him.

"'Tis not the island," repeated the Prince. "Only I know where the real island is, and I will lead you there only as your captain. Now put down your weapons and help me out of this—"

"The head lies," a pirate said. "'Tis *so* the island."

"Aye," said another. "Whoever heard of diverting at one island to find another? Why wouldn't we be sailing right for her?"

"Aye," said the rest. "Why indeed?"

"The chart was not a chart per se," said the Prince, "but indirect directions that misdirect and redirect, to make finding the island difficult even for those possessing them."

"Arrgh," said the pirates again, though this time it suggested confusion and contemplation.

"I say again," said the Prince, "only I can lead you to the island, and I will do so only as your captain. Now put down your weapons and help me."

The pirates muttered and grumbled but seemed ready to comply. Despite his dire circumstances—he was still, after all, driven up to his neck in the deck of a ship full of pirates—the Prince was encouraged, for if the *Bloody-Doodle Doo* did not pass close enough to the island for the pirates to see who lived there, he might successfully lead them astray. And perhaps—dare he hope?—he might even gain time to devise a way of saving himself. "You shall have them," he urged the wavering pirates, "the helpless women and young girls... you want them, don't you?"

"Wait!" said Double-Headed. "Why don't we leave him in his hole and eyeball this island ourselves? If he's telling the truth, and it ain't our pleasure dome—aye, he'll be captain all right, at least until we've found the right island. But if he be lying...."

"I never lie—not anymore," said the Prince. "I am the Prince."

"Aye," said Razors. "But didn't ye tell Slag ye'd changed yer mind? Didn't ye say ye didn't want them women sliced up after all?"

"Aye!" cried the others. "He did say that, he did!"

"I said that only to incite Slag to fight," said the Prince, "so that I might have the honor of leading you to the island myself."

"No," said Razors, "ye wished to deprive us our fun!"

"Lying clack-dish!" said Double-Headed to the Prince. He stepped forward. "I'll kill ye now!" But the others had played this one before. "No I!" they all cried. "No I! No I!" Only now they did not circle and menace and feint, but leapt upon one another in an instant with a great clashing of swords and thudding of bodies and howls of fury and murder. So fast and ferociously did they attack, that whichever way the Prince looked he saw only a slashing blur, a whirlwind of men and glinting weapons, from which flew great gouts of blood and lopped-off body parts. An eyeball hit him in the back of the head; a liver flopped moistly onto the deck beside him; and blood was shed so abundantly that it washed over the Prince in waves and rose in a mist into the sky. And then just as suddenly as it had begun the whirlwind subsided. All grew quiet, and the pirates—every one of them!—lay dead in a ring around the Prince, their hands still clutching blades that were plunged into the breast or back or throat or eye-hole of a mate. And it took the stunned, blood-soaked Prince so long to free himself from the hole in the deck that by the time he did the ship had run aground at the island.

Now, the King's wives and their daughters kept a regular watch on the island, half out of hope that the King would relent and send ships to bring them back to Uaxala, and half out of fear of pirates and marauders, as their only protection from such men was the island's uncharted isolation. But in five years of exile, not a single ship had been sighted—not because no ship had passed by, but because on those rare occasions when one did appear distantly on the horizon, the young girl on watch (for it was to the daughters that this duty fell), not being a disciplined soldier, was fast asleep or not watching. This particular morning, however, the watcher had happened to wake with the sun, and lay peering out to sea, dreaming of her former life as a princess in the palace, which in its luxury and idleness seemed no more real to her now than a fairy tale. And so at about the same moment that "Land ho!" had rung out on the *Bloody Doodle-*

Doo, the girl spied the ship tit-for-tat. She ran to her hut of sticks and fronds and woke her mother, who ran to wake Undine, but found her already awake and gazing tenderly yet forlornly upon her twenty-one sleeping daughters. When Undine was told of the sighting, she started as out of a reverie, and said in a stricken voice, "So soon?"

"What do you mean?" said the other woman, puzzled.

But Undine only sighed heavily and said, "Let us go down to the beach." As word of the ship had spread, they were met there by other worried wives.

"Who is it?" asked the King's wives, squinting at the tiny distant ship. "Can you see? Is it royal?"

"It's pirates," said Undine coolly.

"Pirates!" gasped the King's wives. "How do you know? It's too far away yet to see!"

"I do not have to see," said Undine. "I know. And I know this as well: the Prince leads them."

"Not the Prince!" squealed the King's wives.

"Yes," said Undine, "the Prince, who can nevermore know his mother's love as our daughters do, even in miserable exile."

"But *how* do you know?" pursued some of the wives, while others, who never doubted anything imperious Undine said, burst into tears and sobbed, "He's come to kill us! What shall we do? What shall we do!"

"Go to your hiding places," said Undine. "I will meet him here alone." Consequently, when the *Bloody-Doodle Doo* (recognized by Undine with a little gasp) grounded itself on the reef just beyond the lagoon, and the Prince rowed ashore, he found himself face-to-face with the woman whom for so long he had hated more than anyone in the world. And though the story of the labyrinth and his subsequent dream had persuaded him not to act upon certain impulses regarding her and the others, still he felt these impulses, and strongly, too. If only she had been surrounded by the others—especially by the daughters, all of whom were older than the Prince, but whom he, in his precocious worldliness, could look upon as innocent children. How much easier it would have been to be merciful! And how much misfortune might have been avoided!

The Prince bowed his most condescending bow, and said with pointed impoliteness, "Undine." (He more properly should have addressed her as "Your Majesty," for she was, after all, still Queen.)

"Your Highness," said Undine in tones of lofty indifference. It was as if she had met him in the gardens of the palace, where she had seen him only yesterday or an hour before, as if he had not arrived on the *Bloody Doodle-Doo*... as if she had no reason to fear him.

"You do not seem very surprised to see me," he said.

"I am not," said Undine, peering at his wounds. "Although I wonder what dreadful thing has happened to you."

"Oh, that," said the Prince, who had no idea how awful he looked. "It is nothing—an accident aboard the ship."

"Yes, the ship," said Undine. "I see."

"Yet you do not seem surprised by the *Bloody Doodle-Doo* either," said the Prince.

"I am not," said Undine, "for last night I dreamed of being ravished by a hideous giant, whom I understood to be the captain of that ship. And in this dream I appealed to you for help."

"No!" whispered the Prince.

"Yes," said Undine blandly. "I begged you to help me, but you drew a dagger and cut my throat from ear to ear."

"It cannot be!" whispered the Prince.

"I realized it to be a premonition," said Undine, who, not knowing how closely her dream resembled a portion of the Prince's, believed him to be astonished merely by the dream's foretelling of his arrival. "Although now that you are here, one does not need premonitions to know why."

"Indeed?" said the Prince.

"Indeed," said Undine. She and the Prince

stared icily at one another, although he thought he could discern in her eyes the slightest trace of uncertain agitation—and a trace of this, from Undine, was worth hysteria from any other person.

"Very well," Undine said at last. "I offer myself."

"What?" said the Prince.

"I offer myself. Kill me, torture me, let your pirate friends inflict upon me all the unspeakable horrors they wish, for as long as they wish—and let that satisfy your lust for revenge."

"Actually..." began the Prince, yet Undine did not allow him to finish. To his great astonishment, she fell to her knees before him, and, clinging to his legs (which hurt the broken one), she exclaimed, "I am to blame for what happened! I and I alone, for the others would have done nothing without my example!"

"Undine," said the Prince, "that's not necessary."

But the woman could not be headed. "And certainly our daughters," she raced on, "our sweet young daughters! They were jealous of you, yes, but none wanted to deprive you of your mother! They love their own mothers too well ever to wish that on someone else!"

"Will you listen to me for a moment?" said the Prince in consternation, trying to peel her off. Yet this, too, went unheeded.

"Spare the others!" Undine wailed. "Spare them, I beg you! Take me!" And closing her eyes she threw back her arms and thrust forward her breast for the knife.

To see Undine thus reduced gave the Prince much delight, and as she trembled before him awaiting the worst, he decided to terrify her a little just for fun. There was plenty of time to be noble and forgiving afterwards, and besides, what would be the harm in it, if that was all the harm she would come to?

"Undine," he said gravely.

She trembled with closed eyes.

"Undine," he said again, "open your eyes. Do you mean what you say? That you acknowledge your responsibility for my mother's death, and wish to atone for it with your life?"

"I do," said Undine, "if you promise to spare the others."

"Interesting offer," said the Prince sincerely, forgetting for the moment that he had already decided to spare them, and that even if he hadn't all the pirates—the agents of his revenge—were dead. "Do you make it because you believe it is just and fair, or merely to save the others?"

"Have I not said I am to blame?"

"But do you believe it?" asked the Prince. "Or do you say it to save the others?"

"I believe it, as I have said... and you ought to take me at my word, because I am Queen. But I do say it as well to save them."

"And if I will not promise to spare them?"

"Then I ask you to kill me now anyway," said Undine, "so that I do not have to witness what follows." Again she closed her eyes tightly, and a tear escaped into the corner of each one. These the Prince relished as one would relish the tears of the immortals.

"And what," said the Prince, "if I said I did indeed set out for this island with the intention of doing all of you the worst harm imaginable, but I have had a miraculous change of heart along the way and twice nearly died in defending you?"

"I would say you are lying," said Undine. "I would say it was a trick to lure the others out of hiding."

"And you will not be convinced otherwise?"

"Not so long as that ship is on the reef."

"In that case," said the Prince, taking a folded cloth out of his waistband, "I have something to show you." He opened the cloth, and inside was a golden dagger. "Do you recognize this?" he asked Undine, who gazed upon it.

"I do not," said she. "Should I?"

"It is the dagger my mother used to kill herself."

Undine lowered her eyes.

"I drew it myself from her still-warm breast," continued the Prince, "and kept it near my person all these years, so that no matter what fleet-

ing pleasure I might enjoy, I would always remember what she had suffered. Now I give it to
you, knowing you will know what to do with it."
And so saying he placed it in her hand.

Undine stared down at the dagger for a long
while. Then she glanced at the Prince, who took a
step backward in case she might swipe at him,
and she glanced also at the pirate ship, which
was, to her mind, strangely quiet.

"You will spare them?" she asked in a whisper, not looking up.

"I will," said the Prince truthfully.

"Say, 'I swear by my mother's grave,'" said
Undine.

"I will not," said the Prince.

"Say it!" commanded Undine.

"I swear by my mother's grave," the Prince
said softly.

"If you break your promise," said Undine,
"may you burn forever in Hell's lake of fire,
where probably you are headed anyway."

"Undoubtedly," said the Prince.

Undine closed her eyes once more—for the
last time, for all she knew—and stretching up her
arm held the dagger aloft, pointing down at her
heart.

The Prince, of course, never meant for Undine to kill herself. He meant to stop her at the
last moment, but only after she had experienced
the closest possible approximation to the horror

experienced by his mother. But now, something extraordinary occurred. As Undine made ready for self-impalement and the Prince saw it was time to stop her, he tried to open his mouth to speak but could not. Nor could he reach out to stay her hand. He was paralyzed, exactly as he had been paralyzed while his mother had prepared to stab herself. It was as if the memory of being unable to save her then would not allow him to save Undine now. In another instant Undine would be dead; the dagger-point quivered dangerously in the air, charging itself, as it were, for the plunge. Yet the Prince was powerless. "No!" he wanted to cry out, "no! I was joking! Do not kill yourself!" But he could not even whimper or squeak. Undine was doomed and it would be on his head. Oh, that he had never set out for this damned island! Oh, that he had understood the Fabulist's story a little sooner!

Yet not being able to move, neither could the Prince maintain his balance on one good leg only. He toppled over onto Undine at the very moment she wrenched the knife down toward her heart. It did not find her heart; it found the Prince's back, and his breath went out of him helplessly.

Chapter Four: Every Possible Form of Painful Death

Let us fly now back across the dawn-bright sea, swifter even than the *Bloody Doodle-Doo*, to Uaxala, where the Fabulist and his Manservant languished in a cell in the tower—or rather, where the Fabulist languished in despondency and acquiescence on a pallet, while his Manservant paced excitedly to and fro, as he'd done since they'd been locked in together.

"It's an injustice," said the Manservant forcefully. "To blame you for whatever that rotten Prince is up to—you who only meant to do well by him, who tried his best to talk sense to a senseless spoiled boy—"

"Do be quiet," said the Fabulist, who'd heard this many times during the night.

"But is it your fault he just wouldn't listen? Is it your fault he wasn't smart enough to see what you were getting at?"

"Let it rest," said the Fabulist.

"But what about *them*?" asked the Manservant.

"Who?"

"The King, that's who, and his flock of so-called wise men and advisors! Don't they share any blame for the Prince's conduct and character? After all, they've had more opportunity to shape him than you! They've had years and years, day in and day out, while all you did was tell him a story!"

The Fabulist covered his ears.

"The way they pamper him and pussy-foot around him," continued the Manservant, "it's disgusting. No wonder he's the brat that he is. No wonder he's incorrigible and intractable and rotten. Did I say insufferable? He's that too! Why, he don't need fables; he needs a proper beating!"

"Let it be!" cried the Fabulist. "I beg you!"

"But it's an injustice," persisted the Manservant. "And they claim to be so enlightened here!"

The Fabulist sighed.

"You're too deep for them, sir," said the Manservant. "That's the problem. But you'll show them. You'll show them." The Manservant suddenly stopped pacing. "Say," he went on, a light breaking upon his face, "that's why you're being so quiet, isn't it! You're cooking up a fable that'll shame them for good, one that'll drop them in the dust at your feet, so they won't dare to lay even a finger on you!"

At this the Fabulist turned his face to the

rough stone wall, so that his Manservant would not see how shamed he was by the suggestion that he tell another tale. But the Manservant assumed he had hit upon his master's very plan, and he sat down beside him on the pallet and slapped him on the back. "Good for you, sir!" he said. "I should have known! And here I've been prattling on at you all night, when what you really need is silence to think. Well my lips are sealed from now on; I'm bridled, as they say. Just let me know if there's anything I can do to help. Would you..." and he looked around, "... perhaps you'd like the chamber pot?"

The Fabulist rose and moved to the opposite side of the cell.

"*That's* the old Fabulist!" said the Manservant. "There's the old fire and authority." But the Fabulist's brow knotted up darkly as the Manservant spoke.

"Besides, sir," said the Manservant, hoping to ease his master's mind, "there's no disgrace in what happened here. And even if there were, no one at home need know about it. I certainly won't tell them; you can count on me. So we return in a pillory and painted yellow... you can say the Uaxalans were barbarians—which they are! You could even have their ship seized and its crew thrown in jail. The tables will be turned then, eh? Because you'll be at home where you are loved and respected..." and here the Fabulist snorted,

"... while they'll be the strangers at our mercy."

"I do not wish to go home," said the Fabulist.

"What sir?" said the Manservant.

"I said, I do not wish to go home."

The Manservant was baffled. "But why not?" he asked.

"I do not wish to return to that life," said the Fabulist.

"But your home, sir! Your family! Your loving wife and fourteen children!"

"My family," said the Fabulist wretchedly, "is better off without me."

"But no one need know, sir. And if the Uaxalans air the story... well, who will be believed— you, or them?"

"I care not a fig for who knows the story," said the Fabulist. "Let them all know, let the world know—I do not care! I meant only that I wish to free my family of the burden of me."

"Excuse me, sir?"

"The burden... I am a burden to them. Who needs someone like me around, who preens and struts and imposes his self-styled wisdom on the slightest pretext, whether it's wanted or not?"

"No, sir!" cried the Manservant.

"You saw it yourself in their faces, when we left home a year ago!"

"No, sir!" insisted the Manservant... though he had.

"My wisdom!" spat the Fabulist. "My fables!

What are they but a mishmash of platitudes and commonplaces, dressed up in fancy clothes and powdered wigs? My fables—bah! I am done with them." He turned to face his Manservant and said with fierce conviction, "I swear to you now, I will never tell another fable or story or tale of any kind as long as I live! May God strike me dead if I do—if there be a God, of which I am no longer convinced!"

"Sir," said the Manservant gravely, "I think you're overreacting."

"I am not."

"I know you've experienced a reversal, but—"

"It is not a reversal," said the Fabulist. "Or rather, it is, but a welcome one, for no longer need I carry on in such a fraudulent, flatulent, self-deluded manner. And ridicule, disapprobrium, a pillory, yellow paint—if these are all I have called down upon myself after the life I have led, then by God, I'm getting off easy."

The Manservant stared at him in wonder. "Then... then you intend to do nothing?" he asked.

"Nothing," said the Fabulist with finality.

"You will let them paint you, pillory you, even hang you, without a word?"

"I will."

"Well that's very good for *you*, sir, if that's the way you feel... but what about *me*?"

"You?" asked the Fabulist.

"Yes me! Your servant; your good right hand!"

"But *you* are not in any danger."

"Am I not?" cried the Manservant, springing off the pallet. "Am I not in this cell, just as you are? Did the King not cast me here, too? Did I not, in your defense, admit to inspiring your story?"

"But that's ridiculous. Who would believe that?"

"Believe it or not—here I am!"

"So you are," reflected the Fabulist, beginning to pace as his Manservant had.

"Maybe *you* don't want to go home," said the Manservant, watching him, "but *I* do. *My* wife and children happen to love me! And need me!"

The Fabulist stopped pacing. "I—I didn't know you had children... or a wife," he said.

"Of course you didn't know it," said the Manservant in disgust. "You're not the sort to notice or care. And to think I followed you loyally to this godforsaken place, and stroked you and babysat you and—"

"Babysat me?"

"Yes, and more! I've saved you from yourself since we got here—and now you will do nothing to save me?"

The Fabulist sagged. Only a day before he would have turned purple at such disrespectfulness, but overnight the world had been stood on its head, and disrespect seemed now what he deserved. "Very well," he said quietly. "I will call for the King and I will plead for you. I will convince him that I alone am to blame, while you ought to be released and sent home."

But the Manservant had flung himself back to the pallet and buried his face in his hands. "What's the use," he said bitterly. "We are lost."

"Do not say so," said the Fabulist. "I will speak to them."

"You'll just get it all wrong anyway. We are lost, I tell you—doomed!"

The Fabulist looked on as the Manservant wrung his hands. "I'm sorry," the Fabulist said at last, helplessly.

"It's a little late for that now," said the Manservant.

"Once again, I've been thinking only of myself."

"Old habits die hard."

"You hate me," sniffed the Fabulist.

"What difference does it make?"

"Nevertheless," said the Fabulist, "you've been far kinder to me under difficult circumstances than I ever was to you under easier ones, and I will not forget it. You are trusty and good-hearted and I will do everything I can—short of telling more fables, that is—to see that nothing happens to you."

"Don't bother," said the Manservant. "I'll speak for myself."

"But I must. It's the least I can do." He marched to the cell door and called through the little barred window, "I demand to see the King! My Manservant is held here unjustly!" And so on. In response, three brawny jailers (who looked like giant dwarves or dwarfish giants, if you can imagine such creatures) entered the cell, put a bucket over his head, and tied it in place with itchy horsetails. It took the Manservant most of the morning to undo the knots and get it off.

And so began the Fabulist's and Manservant's time of captivity. On the second day, they asked their jailers hopefully whether the Prince had turned up, or whether word of his whereabouts had been received. This occasioned inscrutable knowing glances among the jailers, one of whom growled, "Wouldn't *ye* like to know!"

On the fifth day, the jailers let into the cell a man who took measurements of every part of their bodies.

"Are we to be dressed as common transports?" the Fabulist protested.

"Oh, I ain't a tailor," the man said ominously. "I'm a carpenter." And that night, a dreadful hammering and sawing began in the great square below the tower. By standing on his tiptoes on the pallet, the Manservant, who was taller than the Fabulist, could peer down through the cell's lone window at this activity.

"What is it?" the Fabulist asked nervously.

The Manservant gulped. "Gibbets," he said. "Gallows, pillories, racks, wheels, whipping posts, dunking chairs and iron maidens." He gulped again. "Two of each."

Noises of construction continued through the fourteenth day, when a proclaimer appeared in the cell and proclaimed the following:

"Whereas the individual currently detained in the tower has amply demonstrated by his weakness of intellect, obtuseness and foolish blundering that he cannot be the *real* teller of tales, celebrated throughout the world for the ingeniousness and moral probity of his fables as well as their ability to entertain, instruct and uplift all at the same time—"

"Not the real Fabulist!" gasped the Fabulist.

"But is in all likelihood an imposter—" continued the proclaimer.

"An imposter!"

"An imposter," repeated the proclaimer, "and whereas the aforesaid individual has by subterfuge, connivances and plots caused the Kingdom of Uaxala to be deprived of its sole Prince and rightful heir—"

"Plots!" said the Fabulist and Manservant together.

"It has been determined," the proclaimer went on, "that the aforesaid individual and his Manservant are agents in the service of a foreign government, specifically the Kingdom of Nearandfar, whose covetousness toward Uaxala is well-known, and further that the aforesaid individual and his Manservant, whomever they may be, have engaged in acts of war and destabilization against the sovereignty and peoples of Uaxala, for which they will be held accountable as spies."

"Spies!" said the Fabulist and Manservant.

"Spies," affirmed the proclaimer, rolling up the proclamation.

"We are to be tried as spies?" said the Manservant.

"Oh no, not tried; you have already been condemned."

"But we were not told!" said the Fabulist. "We weren't present at our trial!"

"Of course not," said the proclaimer. "Why should you be present?"

"But who spoke in our defense?"

"Your defense?" asked the proclaimer, puzzled. "What defense?" And with that he left the cell.

The Manservant turned on the Fabulist. "You fat idiot!" he cried. "You have murdered me!"

"That's not fair!" said the Fabulist, which was true, at least in part, for he was no longer as fat as he used to be, having lost much weight from worry and self-condemnation, and from the diet of breadcrumbs and water lapped by dogs, on which Uaxalan prisoners were maintained.

The Manservant rushed to the cell door and shouted through the window, "Please, I must have my own cell! Please—I cannot bear to look at him!" Minutes later, the Fabulist was tugging quietly at knotted horsetails that bound a bucket to the Manservant's head.

Days fifteen through twenty-eight passed in constant dread that any minute the mortification of their flesh would begin—which perhaps was a part of their punishment. The Manservant spoke as little as possible to the Fabulist, and ignored the many pitiful beseeching looks the Fabulist directed his way. Then, on the twenty-ninth day, the King came to their cell. But he was no longer the clear-eyed, strong-voiced model of healthful agelessness who had greeted the Fabulist upon his arrival in Uaxala. He had withered. He was supported on both sides by attendants, who gently held his stick-like arms at the elbow. His white beard had grown lank and thin; his gaze was cast down at his feet. His ministers, chancellors, viziers and wizards clustered behind him, with expressions of tender concern for their King and fierce enmity for the Fabulist and Manservant.

"Your Majesty," a minister said to the King, who did not seem to know where he was.

"Has little Hal come home?" the King asked weakly.

"Alas, no," said the minister. "But here are

the spies."

"The spies?" said the King. He gazed at the Fabulist, and slowly recognition stole upon him. Then did a glimmer of his former character return. He wrested himself out of the arms of his attendants, and his eyes burned brightly once more.

"You!" he said. "Corrupter of my son! Assassin of my heart! Destroyer of the hopes of my people!"

The Fabulist hung his head meekly.

"Oh, you are clever," the King continued. "You who seemed the stupidest of men—you have proven too clever for us. How you must be laughing! How you must be laughing at *our* stupidity!"

"No, Your Majesty," said the Fabulist. "I am not laughing. I am ashamed and sorry."

"Silence!" roared the King. "Silence forever, I command it!" Yet he tottered so that his attendants hastened to catch him. Meanwhile, his ministers, chancellors, viziers and wizards were so stung by the sight of their enfeebled King that they turned away to wipe tears from their eyes.

"Do you see?" said the King to the Fabulist. "Do you see the fruit of your evil work? We shall avenge ourselves... as the babies in your story were avenged... but nothing... nothing..." He faltered, and the fury in his eyes turned to heartbreak. To the astonishment of all and the chagrin of the Uaxalans, he threw himself upon the Fabulist's neck, and wailed, "Where is he? Where is Hal? Where is my son?"

"Your Majesty!" cried the Fabulist, struggling to hold up the King; and the Manservant, struggling to hold up both, cried "For God's sake, don't drop him!"

"Give him back!" the King wailed piteously. "Oh please! I beg you… give him back to me!"

"Sire!" cried the ministers, chancellors, viziers and wizards, rushing in. But they could not pry him from the Fabulist's neck, for he clung to it as a frightened child clings to its mother—that is, as if for life.

"Have I not lost enough?" sobbed the King. "First dear Toothsome—then *all* my wives and daughters—and now… now…."

Still the ministers, chancellors, viziers and wizards pulled at him with cries of "No, Your Majesty!" and "Come now!" King, Uaxalans, Fabulist and Manservant surged this way and that on scuffling feet, very nearly ending up in a heap on the floor, until the King moaned, "Unhand me!"

All in the cell fell back and were silent. The King drew back from the Fabulist as well, and as the Fabulist watched him attempt to recover himself, he felt he would give his life to reunite the King with his son. Yet simultaneously there was kindled within him a desire to be reunited with his own children, and his wife, to earn their forgiveness and begin anew.

The King now fixed his eyes upon the Fabulist. "I beg you," he said quietly. "Not as a King, not as a sovereign, but as a father who loves his son. Restore him to me! Please! I beg you."

"I would if I could!" said the Fabulist.

"You refuse?" said the King.

"Nay," said the Fabulist, "for how can I refuse what I cannot do?"

"Tell me then, where is he?"

The Fabulist sighed. "I don't know. I wish I did!"

"Has he gone to the island?" said a minister. "We sent a ship immediately, of course...."

"But they don't have the chart!" said another. "It has been stolen! It may take them months to find the island, if they ever do."

The Fabulist hesitated, for a hateful thought now came to him—namely, that he could lie. He could invent a tale, a whopper with many complications, of necessity the greatest of his career, and thereby forestall the horrors the Uaxalans were preparing for him and his Manservant. If he were clever enough, he might even gain his Manservant's freedom. He glanced at his Manservant, who, for the first time since the first night of the reversal of their fortunes, was looking at the Fabulist with something other than hatred.

"That's it!" the Manservant whispered. "Tell them something! Tell them anything!"

The Fabulist quavered in a quandary. If ever there was a time when a tale might be timely, when fabulating might be the right thing to do, that time was now. But what of his vow, made solemnly and forever?

"Go on!" urged the Manservant. "You can do it! You must!"

Against his will the Fabulist felt a familiar inner swelling that foretold the issuance of a story. How natural and comforting it would be to let the words flow as they had always flowed, like music or wine or love. It was the easiest, most natural thing in the world! He opened his mouth and drew a breath. "The Prince..." he began.

The King crept closer. "Yes?" he said anxiously, eyes widening.

"The Prince..." repeated the Fabulist.

"Yes?" said the ministers, chancellors, viziers and wizards, also creeping closer. The Fabulist stared at them, and at his Manservant, who was watching him too. Countless audiences had hung on his words just this way, countless faces just like these had waited for him to say something worth hearing. And what had he given them? Lies and flummery, bombast and rubbish, humbug and twaddle. It sickened him to think of it, for that had been his life. He could not imagine a more wasted or false one. What he had said to his Manservant was true: no more lies, no more tales; he was done with them, even if it meant he must die. Yet he could not allow his Manservant to die. He would have to find a way to save him, but a way that was founded upon Truth. And perhaps by this act, which would be his first of integrity and last on earth, he might redeem a portion of his worthlessness.

"Your Majesty," he said, trying to restrain his customary ostentatious tone so that he might speak as convincingly as possible, "we are not spies or grand manipulators or wirepullers. My Manservant is what he seems: a simple Manservant. And I? I am just a pathetic old man who talks without thinking."

"No!" cried the Manservant. "He's lying!"

"I am not," said the Fabulist. "I would be lying if I pretended to be more."

"No!" said the Manservant. "He's lying *now*!"

"I am not, and never will again," said the Fabulist.

Now it was the Manservant who leapt upon the Fabulist, and seizing him by his sagging jowls, roared into his face, "Tell them! Tell them! The whole story! You must!"

"Hush!" said the Fabulist. "You don't know what you are saying."

"Tell them!" roared the Manservant, wetting

the Fabulist's cheeks with spittle.

"But you are making things worse!" said the Fabulist, eyeing the King, who with his ministers, chancellors, viziers and wizards was following this closely, from Fabulist to Manservant and back again, as one follows the flying shuttlecock in a game of Hit and Scream.

At last the Fabulist shook off the Manservant. "There is nothing to tell," he said, "beyond the sorry tale of my pretension."

"Then I will tell!" said the Manservant.

The Uaxalans' faces lit up. "You are ready to confess?" they asked.

"Confess?" said the Manservant. "Well, that is..."

". the Royal Recorder of Confessions," said the King.

"But wait," cried the Manservant. "I'm not confessing. I haven't done anything wrong! I'm just telling you what *he* did!"

"Then summon the Royal Recorder of Betrayals," said the King.

"Betrayals?" said the Manservant. "But that's not it either!"

"What then?" asked the ministers, chancellors, viziers and wizards.

"I can tell you... I can tell you what has become of the Prince!"

"Oh, do!" cried the King.

But the Fabulist said, "Your Majesty, my

Manservant is frightened and desperate. He wishes to tell you what he thinks you wish to hear. But he does not know where the Prince is any more than I."

"Be quiet!" cried the Manservant. "You have had your chance!"

"Yes, be quiet," said the King. "Go on," he urged the Manservant.

The Manservant faced the Uaxalans who looked to him now as previously they had looked to the Fabulist. He had always considered himself clever—far cleverer, to be sure, than his famous master. Yet always he had whispered his cleverness from the wings, whereas now he was thrust upon the stage. "All right," he said uncertainly, "go on, I will." But how would he go on, and to where would he go? He had no idea, nor even the faintest glimmer of an inkling of a clue. He knew only that he must be very artful. He must convince the Uaxalans that he knew what had happened to their brat of a Prince, and where he now was... yet he could not imply by knowing it that he had conspired with the Hereandthereians or Nearandfarians or whatever they were called, those whom the Uaxalans believed were behind it all. At the same time, he must convince them that he and only he could bring the Prince back, so that it would not serve their interest to torture or kill him. He looked sideways at the Fabulist, who was shaking his head sadly. What would he say in such a situation? He seemed always just to open his mouth, and the words tumbled out as if of their own accord. So that was what the Manservant did.

"The Prince," he said, "is in hiding."

"Hiding?" said the King. "From whom?"

"Actually, he's been kidnapped," said the Manservant.

"Kidnapped!" gasped the Uaxalans, and the King staggered with a hand upon his heart. "Can it be?" he said in anguish. "My Hal?"

"Yes," said the Manservant. "That's it, I'm afraid."

"Nonsense!" said the Fabulist, though none heard him.

"But who?" said the King. "Who would dare?"

"Pirates," said the Manservant, not knowing he had stumbled upon a semblance of the truth.

"Dear God," the King whispered. "is it Slag?"

"I beg your pardon?" asked the Manservant, for being from the other side of the world, he had never heard of this terror of the seas.

"Slag! Slag! Is it him?"

"Why yes, the very one."

"I knew he wasn't dead!" cried the King. "Alas, this is worse than I feared!"

"Preposterous!" said the Fabulist, though his voice was no more heeded than the voice that tells a starving man not to eat too much too quickly.

"But if he has been kidnapped by Slag," asked a vizier, "why has there been no ransom?" And the others, not wishing to be shown up, echoed, "Yes! Why no ransom? Tell us that."

"Ah! You are quick," said the Manservant to gain time to think, for things were moving a little faster than he had expected. "Why indeed?" he said, hoping it sounded deep, and to help this impression along he raised an eyebrow.

"Is ransom not the chief object?" asked a minister.

"Is a more strategic game afoot?" asked another.

"The Nearandfarians?" said a third, who had been the chief proponent of this theory.

"Well no... not precisely," said the Manservant. "Here is what happened: you recall how the Prince left the great hall after the feast which was so disastrous for my master and myself—"

"Yes? Yes?" said the King.

"And you recall," continued the Manservant, "how the Prince said he had an appointment? Well his appointment was with the pirates. You see, the Prince had been planning for a very long time to lead this Snag—"

"Slag," the King corrected.

"Yes Slag... of course—what am I saying? At any rate, the Prince had been planning to lead this brute and his fearsome murderous men to the island of your wives and daughters. There they would rape and murder and slice and pierce and flay and gouge..." and he stabbed at the air as he enumerated these attacks, "...and lop and hack and—"

"Please do not go on so!" said the King.

"Well, you get the idea. The pirates would have their fun, and the Prince would have his revenge."

"I do not believe my son could do such a thing," said the King.

"Nevertheless, that was his plan."

"But what happened? They kidnapped him instead?"

"Er... sort of," said the Manservant. "At the last moment the Prince changed his mind, for your judgment of his character is correct: he could not do such a thing after all, and yet he might have, if not for my master's story."

The Fabulist, who had been trying to ignore these proceedings to take no part in their false-ness, now looked at his Manservant in surprise, and the King looked at *him* in surprise.

"*His* story?" sneered the King.

"Yes. The Prince pondered its themes aboard the pirate ship, as my master hoped he might, and he realized that compassion is more princely than revenge, and he would be just like Queen Undine and the others were he to cause their deaths as they had caused his mother's, and two wrongs don't make a right, and so forth. But the pirates of course had no such scruples, and the Prince had to challenge Slag to fight."

"Hal dueled mighty Slag? Then he is eaten!" wailed the King.

"He is not," said the Manservant, "for impossible as it seems, Hal won the duel and killed Slag."

"But wait," said the King. "You just said Slag was not dead."

"Well he wasn't... but he is now."

At this point a few of the ministers, chancellors, viziers and wizards, who were not so caught up in the Manservant's story as the King understandably was, began to ask themselves a good question, namely, How could the Manservant know all this, since he had been held in the tower since the feast? No doubt you are asking yourself the same question, for you know, as the Uaxalans did not, that the Prince was the only person who could have related it to the Manservant... and yet, he was stabbed on the island and most likely was dead. You might ask yourself a further question as well: How could the Manservant, in attempting to spin a falsehood off the top of his head, have hit upon what really happened? Was magic at work? Or have I, you might ask in irritation, been holding out on you? To the latter question I can answer honestly no; that is, I have been holding out on you no more than any other author, who knows (or ought to know) the end of his story from the very beginning, in order to lead you there in due course. As to the question of magic, I can only shrug and say this is not the first inexplicable element in my story, nor will it be the last. Make of them what you will.

Not pausing to consider whether his story was the proper one to establish his innocence (for he was seized by an inspiration the origin of which seemed otherworldly), the Manservant went on to describe in uncanny detail how the Prince slew Slag by exploding his tattoos; how the pirates killed one another in a fight over who would kill the Prince; how the ship ran aground at the island; how Undine offered herself as a sacrifice; and how the Prince attempted a cruel trick upon her. During this the ministers, chancellors, viziers and wizards exchanged looks of dubiety and impatience. But the King did not notice them, so desperate was he for any news of his son, no matter how unlikely or improbable. Nor did the Manservant notice, as he was carried away on the dreamlike flow of words. Nor did the Fabulist notice, for he felt the reflected heat of the Manservant's invention, and marveled to see from the outside what he had experienced so often from within.

The Manservant now came to the climax of his story, the moment when the paralyzed Prince toppled onto Undine and took the blow which would have killed her. "It did not find her heart; it found his back, and his breath went out of him helplessly," he concluded.

The King burst out into tears. "Hal is dead! He is dead! My brave son!" he sobbed.

Immediately, the Manservant realized his mistake; if the Prince was dead, so would he be, and soon. "Not dead!" he said. "Not dead!"

"No?" asked the King through his tears.

"No... he yet lives, though he totters upon the precipice of death."

"We must save him!" cried the King. He turned to his ministers, chancellors, viziers and wizards. "Why are you standing there? We must move! We must fly to him!"

But the ministers, chancellors, viziers and wizards could not meet his look. "Oh, Sire," they said woefully, "don't you see what he is doing?"

"He is telling us where the Prince is!"

"But Sire," they said. "How can he know all this about the Prince? He has been here in this cell, and the Prince is... wherever, far away."

The King stared at them.

"He is lying," said the ministers, chancellors, viziers and wizards.

"No!" cried the Manservant.

"He is lying to save his skin," said the ministers, chancellors, viziers and wizards.

"You mean...?" said the King.

"Yes," said the ministers, chancellors, viziers and wizards. "He is telling a tale."

"No! That's not so!" cried the Manservant. But the logic of it was irrefutable, even to a King in a state of heartsick befuddlement. The vigor and authority he had seemed to regain rushed out of him; brightness left his eyes, and hope fled his face. He would have fallen to the floor if his attendants had not caught him. Quickly, they carried him from the cell, and the ministers, chancellors, viziers and wizards filed out after.

"But wait!" the Manservant called to them. "I'm not lying! I'm telling the truth!" Which he was, though he did not know it, but he felt it in some inexplicable way.

The ministers, chancellors, viziers and wizards withered him with looks of disdain.

"All right: I was lying," the Manservant said. "But I'm ready to tell the truth now!"

The last Uaxalan stopped in the doorway. "The Grand Inquisitor shall extract the truth," he said ominously, and pulled shut the cell door behind him.

The Manservant covered his face with his hands.

"There, there," said the Fabulist. "You have tried your best, which was quite good, I must say. But you see that lies have gained us nothing."

"Then why didn't you stop me?" cried the miserable Manservant. "Or help me? You could have helped!"

"I told you," said the Fabulist. "I have made a vow to live honestly for as long as I have left."

"Bah!" spat the Manservant. "You are as self-ish in your pretensions to honesty as you were in your former falseness!"

"Now, now," said the Fabulist. "You are hot, I know—"

"Your vow! What do I care for your vows? I care about my life, you fool! My life and my family!"

"Don't despair," said the Fabulist. "As long as there is breath we may hope, may we not?"

"Shut up!" snarled the Manservant. He was panting, and his eyes blazed fiercely. His fists clenched and shook, and his mouth quivered. "If I said before that I hated you," he went on in a low voice and with difficulty, "I was wrong. For I didn't know what hate was until now."

The Fabulist sighed. "And you are justified, I am sure," he said. "But listen. I do not care about myself, but I promise you this: you shall not die here."

"But *you* will," said the Manservant, turning red in his face and white at his knuckles. "I'll kill you myself!"

"That is the voice of your despair," said the Fabulist. "But I have gotten you into this, and I shall get you out. I don't yet know how, but I will convince the Uaxalans of their error, at least in regard to you, and they will release you and send you home. This I promise you: I give you my word."

"Why should anyone believe *your* word?" said the Manservant, and the Fabulist fell silent, for he could not think of a single reason.

That night, the hammering in the square resumed twice as energetically as before. The Fabulist lay awake in a corner of the cell, racking his brain for a way to save his Manservant. Yet perhaps because of a lifetime of habit, all he hit upon was lies and nonsense, such as, the Prince had been in league with the Fabulist from the beginning, to teach his father the King a lesson (but what?) or the Prince had gone into hiding out of embarrassment at his former behavior. These were insipid notions that led nowhere, and the Fabulist would have snapped his fingers at them even had he not resolved not to lie. The Truth shall carry all before it, he told himself. But how he might present the Truth to best advantage— how he might clear the way for it, so to speak— this he did not know, nor could he tease it out of his tired brain. At last he fell asleep to brood upon the problem in dreams.

Meanwhile, upon the pallet, the Manservant gazed at the moon, which shone palely through the cell's high window. Yet he did not see it, for tender pictures of his home and family passed before his eyes. Perhaps at home, on the other side of the world, it was morning, and his wife was just rising from their bed, her face red and warm from sleep and her hair falling softly upon her neck. Or perhaps it was bedtime, and she was bending to kiss their three children—the twins Blaise and Benno, and tiny Casimir. "When is Poppa coming home?" they might ask her, their covers pulled up to hide the tears in their eyes. "He's been gone so long… we miss him!"

"Soon," his wife would whisper. "Now go to sleep and you will see him in your dreams."

Suddenly, he felt as if they *could* see him, as if they hovered above him near the ceiling of his cell.

"Poppa," they said with troubled faces, "what is this dark place you are in? Why do you linger here when you ought to be coming home to us?" The Manservant groaned with longing.

"Come down," he called, "that I may hold you one last time!"

His children floated toward him, but as he gathered them in his arms, they vanished like the specters they were. "Farewell!" he whispered. "Mind your mother."

Turning away the Manservant saw the Fabulist in his corner across the cell. That he could sleep—and snore so loudly, too—while the Manservant was tormented with visions! It was intolerable. The Fabulist's mortification, the tearing of his flesh and the slow letting out of his life, was not enough—or rather, it might be enough for the Uaxalans, but not for the Manservant.

The Manservant rose from the pallet and knelt by the Fabulist. Here in the corner it was dark; the Manservant could see only the Fabulist's dark shape. Gently, he felt for the Fabulist's throat and placed his hands around it. The Fabulist stirred but that was all... and the Manservant began to squeeze. The Fabulist's breathing became rough and gasping, and after a moment he awakened in confusion and alarm. His hands flew up to the Manservant's hands, yet he could not break their grip, nor even slow their tightening, so implacably did the Manservant squeeze. Then the moon in its passage across the high window cast a ray onto where they grappled, and their faces were lighted up for the other to see.

Now it is widely known that murder is easy in the dark but hard in the light, for the light shows us our wickedness all too plainly. So it was that the Manservant blenched when he saw his hands around the Fabulist's throat, and his grip for a moment was loosened. Yet the Fabulist did not try to break away. Instead he grew strangely quiet, and this was because he saw in the Manservant's eyes not hatred and vengefulness, but infinite, unendurable sorrow—not self-sorrow, either, but sorrow for those he loved. "You may kill me," the Fabulist croaked. "I am ready to die if you wish it. But hadn't you ought to allow me the opportunity to do so for your benefit?"

A sob escaped the Manservant and he flung himself back to the pallet and hid his face.

The Fabulist coughed and cleared his throat. In a hoarse whisper, but gently, he said out of the darkness (for the moon, having done its good work, had passed on), "My friend, are you awake? I have had a very bad dream."

"So have I," said the Manservant without lifting his head.

"Fortunately," said the Fabulist, "bad dreams fade upon awakening. Yet I will try to retain one element of it, in which I felt I understood you better than ever had before."

"Perhaps I... understand you a little better, too," said the Manservant.

"Try to sleep now," said the Fabulist. And they might have been able to if not for the infernal hammering and sawing in the square. As it was they were awake when their giant dwarf or dwarfish giant jailers came for them at dawn.

The Manservant, who after such a night ought not to have had much energy, led the jailers in a lively chase about the cell. He dashed for the door, the high window and the door again, and scrambled over the pallet and under it, and cowered behind the Fabulist, all the while exclaiming, "Let me go! We'll pay you! It's a dreadful mistake!" The jailers seemed to enjoy this for a while, lunging at the Manservant and letting him slip from their clutches as a cat lets slip a mouse. Yet when they grew tired, they caught him without much difficulty (or gentleness, for that matter). Clucking happily, they fixed iron rings about the Fabulist's and Manservant's ankles, and threaded the rings together with heavy chains. The Manservant was reduced to a feeble last appeal: "I'm an innocent man with three small children! Let me go for their sake if not for mine!" But the jailers were fatalists, as demonstrated by the brawniest and most deformed of the three who recited to the Fabulist and Manservant, "'I hold the world but a stage,' as that there poet said, 'where every man must play a part, and yours a sad one.'"

"Sad fer them maybe," said the second jailer.

"But divertin' for us," said the third, who was grinning.

"God save us!" whimpered the Manservant.

"Be stalwart," said the Fabulist. But as they descended with clanking chains the long winding staircase from the tower, the Manservant's legs failed so that the Fabulist had to support him. His head lolled on the Fabulist's shoulder, and he murmured crackbrained things such as "Don't tease your sister!" and "Look—you've made Casimir cry!"

"Dear man!" said the Fabulist, much affected. "Sweet man!"

"Look—what's in my pocket?" said the Manservant. "Chocolates—three! One for each!"

"Dear sweet man!" said the Fabulist, kissing his Manservant's forehead. He tried to remember whether he'd ever given chocolates to his children. No; he'd stuffed them instead with lessons, morals, precepts and false truisms, when there was more love in a chocolate than all of those. Was it any wonder they felt no love for him? And now it was too late to make amends. Perhaps, even if he were to see them again, perhaps it would still be too late. "Forgive me, Marmion, Cathecta, Cicero, Melpomone, Hepsiba, Coriolanus, Aesop, Virgil, Virgilio, Tertullian, Robert," (his wife had picked that one) "Laphronia, Attracta, Sophocles and..." who was he forgetting? "...oh yes: Ffrenchmullan," he whispered. "Don't be to your children as I was to you."

"Step lively," growled one of the jailers.

"Brute!" said the Fabulist.

Toward dawn he had been preparing an appeal for mercy for his Manservant. "Noble enlightened Uaxalans," he had planned to begin (if he should be allowed to speak, that is), yet now his ire rose at the thought of his Manservant being tortured and murdered so pointlessly. "Monsters of cruelty!" he saw himself denouncing the Uaxalans, "Pursuers of unexampled injustice!" He would cast them into a rhetorical pit with the horrid tyrants of history, with Herod the First who ordered all the children in Bethlehem to be killed and who murdered his own wife; with Epiphanes who ordered Ulpianus to be scourged and then fastened up in a sack with a dog and a venomous snake and thrown into the sea; with Diocletianus, who burned 20,000 Christians in the Church of Nicodemia, or with Urbanus, Governor of Palestine, who handed virgin girls over to brothels and had young men castrated for use as pathics; and, most tellingly perhaps, with the tyrant of tyrants Caligula, who ran out of guilty persons to torture and chose innocent victims at random. And if that did not shame the Uaxalans, then they had no shame, and the Fabulist would do his best to resist, delay and frustrate them, for who knew what might happen or what he might think of along the way?

"Here now, stop that," he said to one of the jailers who was prodding him in the back to hurry.

"I'll tumble ye, spy!" said the jailer.

Then should it become necessary to "confess"—and if by doing so, he could gain the release of his Manservant, or (he gulped) gain him the release of swift death—then so be it. He would do it. He would lie, or even fabulate at greater or lesser length, though not for self-aggrandizement as he had always fabulated before, but to save a good man's life. For he saw now that solemn vows should be kept not in and

of themselves, but only as long as they impelled
us toward the good, and they should not be kept
if there was no goodness in them.

"The master?" murmured the Manservant,
still in the throes of delirium. "A horse's ass!"

"There, there," said the Fabulist. "Save your
breath."

At last they reached the bottom of the stairs
and emerged into the square and brilliant sun-
shine. At their appearance a great roar went up,
which made the Fabulist tremble, and aroused
the Manservant from his fever-dreams, for as-
sembled there were thousands upon thousands
of Uaxalans—the high, the low, and all in between; men, women and children, the very same
people who only one short month ago had turned
out on the docks to welcome the Fabulist so
warmly. Now, however, as the Fabulist and
Manservant rode in a cart through the midst of
this vast concourse, they were showered with
rocks, sticks, rotting vegetables and stinking offal;
aged crones spat at them and bared their withered teats; men cursed and shook their fists;
mothers hid their babies' faces, so they would not
be deformed or blighted from seeing the prisoners; and maidens fainted. Slowly the cart rolled
along, the Fabulist and Manservant cowering
inside, to the far end of the square where a large
platform had been erected. Upon this waited the
King in a rolling invalid chair; his ministers,

chancellors, viziers and wizards; priests and cardinals of the Uaxalan church; and bare-armed executioners in black hoods. Ranged about the platform were the gibbets, gallows, pillories, racks, wheels, whipping posts, dunking chairs, iron maidens and many other less well-known but even more dreadful engines of torture soon to be described in detail, the noises of whose construction had disturbed the Fabulist and Manservant in their cell.

The Fabulist and Manservant were pulled roughly from the cart to the platform, and the Uaxalan Grand Inquisitor stepped towards them. He was tall, gaunt, black-robed; his eyes were deep and black-circled and he wore a stiff black moustache which wasn't actually a moustache, but his nose hairs grown long and waxed to points. In one arm he held the Uaxalan Holy Book, a strange and powerful volume read with a mirror back to front, to make time run backwards to the sinless state of earthly paradise; in the other he held the peculiar Uaxalan cross, which was enclosed in a ring in a star, and the star was enclosed in a pentagon and the pentagon in a hexagon and the hexagon in a heptagon and so on up to decagon so that, all in all, it didn't look much like a cross. The Grand Inquisitor circled this relic above the heads of the Fabulist and the Manservant, and then held it out toward the crowd.

"What is God's will?" said the Grand Inquisitor, and though he spoke to a flat open space, his voice echoed as if it sounded from a cave or a hole.

"Ask the King!" the crowd intoned as one. The Grand Inquisitor turned to the King, but the King was unawares.

"Your Majesty," said the Grand Inquisitor.

"What?" said the King, looking up. "Has little Hal come home?"

"Alas, no," said the Grand Inquisitor. "But your people ask, what is God's will?"

The King peered about, then his eyes found the Fabulist and Manservant. "Oh, it's them," he said sadly. "Proceed."

The Grand Inquisitor addressed the Fabulist and Manservant. "The determinations of unerring Uaxalan justice having been proclaimed to you, namely that you—"

"Excuse me," said the Fabulist.

The Grand Inquisitor stared at him a moment in distaste, then began again: "The determinations of unerring Uaxalan justice having been proclaimed to you, namely that you—"

"Excuse me," said the Fabulist once more. His Manservant nudged him fearfully to be quiet, and a murmur ran through the crowd.

Again the Grand Inquisitor stared, though not in distaste as before, but incredulously. "Are you *interrupting* me?" he asked in his echoing voice.

"Forgive me," said the Fabulist. "I only wish to know when I shall be given a chance to say a few short words."

"During each excruciation you will be asked three times to confess," said the Grand Inquisitor. "Three times will you be asked—"

"In my country," said the Fabulist, "it is traditional to give condemned men a last word."

"You are not *in* your country," said the Grand Inquisitor. "You are in ours."

"But it is traditional in many other countries, too," the Fabulist persevered. "In fact, I have never heard of a country that does not follow this civilized tradition. The principle, I imagine, is that since the condemned will be dead soon anyway, there is no harm in letting him say whatever is on his mind. Now that I think about it, many countries, including my own, go even farther in allowing the condemned a last meal of his choosing. Not that I am hungry — far from it…" and so on and so forth, blah blah blah.

During this disquisition, the Grand Inquisitor signaled one of the executioners, who came forward with an iron framework in the shape of a helmet. "This," said the Grand Inquisitor, interrupting the Fabulist, "is a branks, or scold's bridle. You can see that it offers no obstruction to the sight, or to the movement of anything other than the tongue, which is silenced by a spar of iron which projects into the mouth as a gag—an exceedingly uncomfortable and cruel gag at that. We shall remove it only when you signify your readiness to confess, or as it interferes with the torture apparatus."

"You wouldn't," said the Fabulist, eyeing the branks.

The Grand Inquisitor waved his hand and the executioner clapped the branks onto the Fabulist's head and tied it in place with horse-tails, of which the Uaxalans seemed to have an unlimited supply. Roughly, they forced the iron gag into the Fabulist's mouth. Instantly the Fabulist realized the Grand Inquisitor was right — the branks *was* uncomfortable and cruel. The rusty iron spar lacerated his tongue and reached almost to the back of his throat, making him choke.

"Do *you* have anything to say?" the Grand Inquisitor asked the Manservant.

The Manservant shook his head.

"Very well. I will continue. The determinations of unerring Uaxalan justice having been proclaimed to you, namely that you are spies, imposters, deceivers and subversives, your confessions will now be sought along with intelligence we believe you to possess, namely the whereabouts or fate of His Royal Highness the Prince, may God shield him."

"The Prince—may God shield him!" sounded the citizens of Uaxala.

"You see about you," continued the Grand Inquisitor, nodding at the machines on the platform, "various apparatuses designed to secure confessions and intelligence that would otherwise be withheld."

"And they kill you, too!" shouted a wit from the crowd, which caused laughter.

"It might interest you to know," said the Grand Inquisitor, "that our King in his farseeing mercifulness," and here he bowed to the King who was shooing a fly, "had abolished these apparatuses long ago, so that they had to be rebuilt for this occasion. We shall now apply you to them one by one, with great skill and science for maximum effect, yet without actually causing you to die. But first, to heighten your mental agonies by the torture of anticipation, I shall catalogue them for you in all their horribleness.

"Here," he said, an unmistakable note of fondness in his voice, "are gibbets, gallows, pillories, racks, wheels, whipping posts, dunking chairs, and iron maidens with pointy embraces, all of which need no explanation. I simply note them so you will note them.

"Here," he went on, indicating a table on which rested a heavy piece of iron and a pile of rocks, "is the Torture of *Peine Forte et Dure*, or Pressing to Death. This iron is placed anglewise across the heart, and the rocks are added until the victim confesses or is crushed, though we shall stop before that point, to preserve you for further tortures.

"Here," he said, indicating a gibbet hung not with a noose but with ropes through pulleys, "is the Torture of Squassation, or the Pulley, which is similar to the Torture of the Rack, or Wooden Horse, but more advanced. These ropes are fastened to the victim's wrists and he is drawn up to a height of six feet off the floor. Hundred-pound weights are attached to the irons on his feet, and he is whipped. Failure to confess is the signal for the torture to start in real earnest. The executioners pull on the ropes, raising the victim almost to the gibbet. Suddenly allowing the ropes to slack for several feet, they abruptly terminate the rapid descent before the weights can reach the floor, jarring every bone, joint and nerve in the body. In most cases, this results in dislocation. The process is repeated again and again until the victim confesses or becomes unconscious."

"Mother!" gasped the Manservant, wide-eyed.

"Hmm? Did you say something?" asked the Grand Inquisitor mildly.

The Manservant shook his head.

"I thought not," said the Grand Inquisitor. "Here," he went on, indicating a life-sized bronze bull, "is the Torture of the Brazen Bull, the invention of a man named Perilaus. Certainly it is one of the most ingenious and diabolical instruments ever conceived by the mind of man." How the eyes of the Grand Inquisitor shone as he said this! "The interior forms a hollow chamber, and there is a trap door in the back. The victim is shut up inside the bull and a fire kindled underneath... and as he is slowly roasted, his roars and screams of agony are transformed, by means of a clever arrangement of flutes in the bull's nostrils, into a melodious lowing. Perilaus himself was the first victim of this instrument, so abominable was it deemed by the king to whom he had presented it.

"Here," continued the Grand Inquisitor, stroking a pair of interlocking iron hoops, "is the Torture of the Scavenger's Daughter. The victim is forced into a kneeling posture, and told to draw in his limbs to compress himself to the smallest possible size. The executioner, having passed one of the iron hoops under the victim's legs, kneels upon his shoulders, forcing his body downwards until the second hoop may be fastened over the small of his back. The agony which the victim suffers is beyond all endurance, and in most cases a confession is obtained before the expiration of the time (one and a half hours) allotted for confinement. Long before this blood spurts from the nostrils, the mouth and the anus—and even, on occasion, from the hands and feet."

On and on went this dreadful catalogue, to the Torture of Boiling, the Torture of Branding, the Torture of Castration, the Torture of Crucifixion, the Tortures of Flagellation and Flaying, the Torture of Hurling from a Tower, the Torture of "Little Ease," the Torture of Mutilation, the Torture of Scalping, the Torture of Stoning, the Torture of the Bath, the Torture of the Pendulum, the Torture of "Iron Gauntlets," the Torture of the "Dice," the Torture of the Frying Pan, the Torture of Water, the Torture of Rats in a Pot, the Torture of the Thumbscrews, the Torture of the "Virgin Mary," the Torture of the Glove, the Torture of the Boots, the Torture of the "Spanish Boot," the Torture of Toxification, and more. The description of each drew *oohs* and *ahs* from the crowd of Uaxalans, though some were tender-hearted and cried, "Mercy!" but were shouted down. The ministers, chancellors, viziers and wizards listened impassively, while the King hummed and picked lint from his robes.

And what of the Fabulist and Manservant? The Manservant shook; his knees grew weak; his mouth dried up; fear squeezed his heart, and he fainted and was revived four times. The Fabulist, however, appeared unmoved. More than that, as the Grand Inquisitor rhapsodized his craft, the Fabulist seemed to acquire an air of indifference or even scorn (or as much of these as one can communicate through a branks), as if to say, "Humph! I am not impressed."

"And if after all this," the Grand Inquisitor

summed up, "you have not told what we wish to know, although this I assure you would be impossible, we shall start all over again, as often as necessary, employing the finest healing arts to keep you alive and conscious. There shall be no escape in death until we have achieved our purpose. And then death, when it comes—gruesome though it will be, for here are the dismembering knives, the disemboweling knives, and the potties to receive the liver, the kidneys, the lungs, appendix, duodenum, etc.—death will seem the sweetest of lovers."

The Grand Inquisitor smiled. "But we are not savages," he said. "You may spare yourselves these ordeals, but not death of course, by confessing before we begin. Remove the branks."

As this was being done the Manservant fell to his knees. "I confess!" he cried. "I confess, I confess—I confess!"

"To what do you confess?" asked the Grand Inquisitor.

"To everything! To anything! To whatever you wish!"

"Where is the Prince?"

"I don't know!" sobbed the Manservant.

"Prepare him," said the Grand Inquisitor. Meanwhile the Fabulist, freed of the branks, was massaging his tongue.

"And you?" asked the Grand Inquisitor. "Do you confess your crimes before God?"

The Fabulist glanced at him but did not respond.

"Do you confess your crimes before God?" the Grand Inquisitor repeated. "Once more shall I ask."

"I confess nothing," said the Fabulist contemptuously. "Furthermore, I am disappointed by your display of equipment."

The Grand Inquisitor blinked. "What?" he asked.

"Your equipment, sir," said the Fabulist. "Most disappointing."

"Disappointing?" said the Grand Inquisitor.

"Certainly," said the Fabulist. "Where is your neck-stretcher? Your tooth-puller? Your arm-knotter?"

"Arm-knotter?"

"Yes—and your back-cracker, your skull-bombs and your calcinator?"

"Calcinator?" said the Grand Inquisitor. He looked at his executioners, who shrugged their shoulders helplessly. "What is a calcinator?" he asked the Fabulist.

"Oh come now. You are joking."

"Perhaps I know it by another name," said the Grand Inquisitor. "Describe it"

"A calcinator," said the Fabulist, "powders the bones within, without disturbing the flesh or organs of the victim. He becomes, in effect, a living sack with no support beyond the muscles."

"Remarkable!" said the Grand Inquisitor.

"Indeed—but it is equally remarkable you do not have one. It was my impression that every Grand Inquisitor worth his name did."

"No," said the Grand Inquisitor regretfully. "But I shall get one! I shall get two!"

"In that case, be sure to pick up an abominatrix, a set of crash cups, and an inflator as well," said the Fabulist. "Because what you have here... why, these toys couldn't make a little girl confess!"

"Oh, really?" said the Grand Inquisitor.

"A sadly unimaginative collection," said the Fabulist, shaking his head. "Though Uaxala has amply demonstrated to me that it leads all other nations in the natural sciences, the arts, and governance, I wouldn't give two straws for you as torturers."

"Is that so!" said the Grand Inquisitor. "I suppose you are an expert on the subject?"

"Not at all. One needs no expertise to see you are lacking."

The crowd stirred at this, and shouted exhortations such as "Big talker!" and "Try him out!" and "He insults us!" and "Make him eat his words!"

"Oh, Master!" whimpered the Manservant, still on his knees. "Why are you enflaming them?"

But the Fabulist ignored him. "Third rate, at

best," he said to the Grand Inquisitor. "And that's being generous."

"Perhaps we should begin then," said the Grand Inquisitor, "so you may evaluate our skills from a standpoint of more familiarity."

"As you wish," said the Fabulist. "Bring forth your sensitizer."

"My... what?" asked the Grand Inquisitor.

"Your sensitizer," said the Fabulist. "Let's get started!"

The Grand Inquisitor bit his lower lip.

The Fabulist looked at him in disbelief. "Don't tell me you don't use a sensitizer," he said.

"What is that?"

"It is exactly as it sounds: a device for sensitizing the victim's nerves, so that whatever tortures follow, the victim is a thousand times more susceptible to their agonies."

"Absurd!" said the Grand Inquisitor. "But... tell me more."

"It is said that the sensitizer is so effective, the most excruciating torture of all is the brushing of the skin lightly with a feather... or the employment of carnal touches that bring such exquisite pleasure, they are unbearable."

"Rubbish!" said the Grand Inquisitor.

"Certainly not. I'm no expert, as I said, but I hear it's all very scientific."

"But you have seen one of these devices?"

"Not in use."

"But you know approximately how it works?"

"Approximately. It is based upon the principle of reversal, in which less becomes more and pleasure becomes pain. The five senses are exposed to a series of very faint stimuli—a tiny pinprick, an inaudible noise, the merest ghost of a flavor, and so on—and the body, in straining to detect them, raises its sensitivity to the nth."

"You mean, like the homeopathic theory of opposites?" asked the Grand Inquisitor.

"Precisely," said the Fabulist. "The basis is quite sound if you think about it, for when the senses are over-stimulated, they become dulled; whereas a minute stimulus... "

"...produces an inversely large response!" cried the Grand Inquisitor. He tapped the points of his nose hair moustaches. "Ingenious," he mused. "But preposterous. Such a device could never be built."

"Quite to the contrary," said the Fabulist. "One simply assembles the proper—"

"No!" cried the Manservant, who had been listening to the Fabulist with growing astonishment. "Are you mad? What are you doing?"

The Fabulist looked at him blankly.

"Don't you see?" said the Manservant. "You are helping them make our tortures a thousand times worse!"

The Fabulist struck his forehead. "Dear God, he is right!" he exclaimed.

"Silence him!" said the Grand Inquisitor to his executioners, meaning the Manservant. But before they could grab him, he tackled the Fabulist and began raining blows upon his head and body.

"Betrayer!" he roared, thumping the Fabulist soundly. "Judas! Reptile!"

"Oof! Ow! Stop!" wailed the Fabulist, and they tumbled about the platform to the great delight of the Uaxalans, who laughed and shouted encouragement. Meanwhile, the executioners were trying to pluck off the Manservant. But the Fabulist had gotten a good grip on him, and as they rolled this way and that underfoot of the ministers, chancellors, viziers, wizards, Grand Inquisitor and other notables, he whispered in the Manservant's ear, "Don't be a fool! There's no such thing as a sensitizer!"

"Yet another lie?" shrieked the Manservant. "You lie with every breath!" And he freed his hand for a great clout on the Fabulist's nose.

"Ow!" said the Fabulist, seeing stars. But he persisted. "I'm trying to save us!" he hissed.

"Incorrigible wretch!" impugned the Manservant. "I'll stop your lies!" He summoned another crushing blow, and another, and another, so that the Fabulist had no choice but to incapacitate his servant with a *coup de l'aine*, or blow to the groin, delivered with the knee. Immediately the Manservant went slack and began to moan. Yet in the moment before the executioners lifted them to their feet, the Fabulist murmured to him, "You must follow my lead closely in this sensitizer thing, and say nothing to contradict me or cause suspicion, for then we are done for. Do you hear?"

The Manservant in his agony gave no indication that he had.

"*There is no such thing as a sensitizer,*" the Fabulist whispered urgently. "I am making it up to save us!" But again the Manservant showed no understanding... unless groans and gaspings for breath were meant as signs to that effect. Very well, the Fabulist decided. He would just have to forge ahead, and assume his Manservant would follow. It was, as far as it went, their only hope.

"You were saying...?" the Grand Inquisitor said mildly to the Fabulist.

"You'll get no more help from me," said the Fabulist disconsolately as he rubbed the bruises and knots that were coming out on his head. "I see now that by playing upon my natural tendency to lecture, you have tricked me into revealing the secret of the sensitizer, so that it may be turned upon myself. Oh, surely there has never been so great a fool as I! But thank God my Manservant stopped me before I gave you sufficient direction."

"Then you *do* know how it operates," said the Grand Inquisitor.

"I do. I have already said too much. Fortunately, your skills as a penologist are so limited, you will never extrapolate the rest."

"You are confident of that?"

"You have shown me nothing to make me think otherwise."

"What impudence!" said the Grand Inquisitor. "I almost admire you." He turned to confer with the ministers, chancellors, viziers and wizards. During this the Fabulist tried to catch his Manservant's eye, but the poor man had not yet opened either one. "Oh, that was dirty!" the Manservant muttered. "A low blow... I might have known!"

"Uaxalans!" the Grand Inquisitor now called, having finished with the ministers, chancellors, viziers and wizards. "There shall be a short delay as we prepare a new device!"

The crowd voiced its displeasure, but as word spread outward from the platform of the wondrous new torture to be used, a hush of anticipation descended. The carpenter who had measured the Fabulist and Manservant in their cell was called to the platform. He spoke briefly with the Grand Inquisitor, then left the platform only to return a moment later with his apprentices carrying a cabinet large enough for a man to fit inside. They commenced to hammer and saw upon its lid, and in a short time had constructed there a shallow compartment, which revolved at the turn of a crank. Into this compartment was placed: a hummingbird hatched not more than five minutes before, and so tiny that when it opened its mouth to peep, only another just-hatched hummingbird might hear it; a single glowing diatom from the bottom of the sea, so faint in its efflorescence that even in those inky depths it was nearly impossible to detect; a rose that had withered more than 2000 years ago, used now by the royal *parfumeur* to test the acuteness of his nose; a saltlick, if such a lick still deserves to be called salt, for a solitary grain of that mineral was dissolved in ten parts pure rainwater, and a tenth of that solution was diluted in ten further parts, and a tenth in ten *further* parts, and so on ten times with vigorous shaking at each stage, the result being painted onto the lick; and a golden downy hairlet plucked from just below the navel of one of the palace's pretty handmaids, which would bend instantly upon pricking the skin so that the skin might be said to have pricked the hairlet instead.

As the Fabulist watched this last item being placed carefully into its slot in the revolving compartment, he gasped, "The very technique of Torquemada! We are undone!" And the Manservant, perhaps getting into the spirit of deception or perhaps he was merely still enraged, abused the Fabulist with convincing vigor either way, shouting at him, "Wicked Janus! Talking ape!" He tried again to attack the Fabulist, and was restrained by the black-hooded executioners.

"So," said the Grand Inquisitor, "the jackals turn on one another once more, as jackals are known to do. Which jackal shall be first in the sensitizer?"

"Please, I beg you," said the Fabulist, "we have nothing to tell. Neither I nor my Manservant—"

"Who shall be first?" demanded the Grand Inquisitor.

"Him," said the Fabulist, pointing at the Manservant.

"No!" cried the Manservant.

"How predictable," said the Grand Inquisitor to the Fabulist. "For that, we'll take you."

"Alas, it is fitting," moaned the Fabulist, "since it is by my stupidity that you have built your sensitizer."

The Grand Inquisitor signaled the executioners, who opened the door of the sensitizer that was until recently merely a cabinet, and into it they bundled the Fabulist. "Careful, careful," the Grand Inquisitor said. "Don't upset the delicate specimens." When the door had been closed he put his head near it and said in his normal echoing voice, "Can you hear me in there?"

There was no response from inside the sensitizer.

"I say," said the Grand Inquisitor, louder, "can you hear me?"

Still there was no response.

The Grand Inquisitor rapped his knuckles on the door, and shouted, "You in there—can you hear me?"

"You'll have to speak up," called the Fabulist from within. "It's hard to hear you in here."

"I said..." said the Grand Inquisitor, "...never mind." One of the executioners had taken the crank, but the Grand Inquisitor waved him off. "I shall do it myself," he announced. "No doubt, great skill is required to apply the sensitizer just enough to leave the body in its heightened state, but not so much that the nerves become jaded." He paused for a moment to admonish the crowd that absolute silence was necessary... and then, with an enthusiast's gleam in his eye, he turned the crank slowly. One time 'round he revolved the compartment atop the cabinet, and that was all. He listened with his ear to the door and yet heard nothing, so he turned the crank again, two times 'round this time. During this second revolution (which was the third revolution over all, if you are counting), the Fabulist was heard to say "Ow!" inside the cabinet, presumably because he'd been pricked by the soft navel down of the handmaid. The Grand Inquisitor now whispered at the door, "Hello?"

"Stop that shouting!" cried the Fabulist behind the door. "Are you trying to deafen me?" From this, we may conclude that while the Fabulist may have been obtuse, he was not exactly *stupid*.

The Grand Inquisitor opened the door of the sensitizer, and the Fabulist cowered back from the sun. With his hands over his eyes he whimpered, "By God, my throat is parched with salt. I must have water! And what's that awful smell? Are you unclean?"

"Quick," said the Grand Inquisitor to his executioners, "the other one." Yet the Manservant backed away from the cabinet uncertainly, for though he had in fact heard what the Fabulist had said about there being no such thing as a sensitizer, he did not know what to believe now. The Fabulist appeared to have emerged from the cabinet a trembling raw nerve who shrank from any sort of contact or sensation. "Ouch!" he cried to the executioner who held his arm gently. "You're breaking my bones with that grip!" Either his master was a much better actor than the Manservant would have supposed, or there was something to this sensitizing business after all.

"Quickly, quickly," said the Grand Inquisitor. "We don't know how long the effect will last."

"Quiet!" cried the Fabulist. "Oh my poor

ears!" But in covering his ears with his hands, he exposed his eyes to the sun, and in covering his eyes he exposed his ears, and so on, so that his hands flew back and forth as if he could not decide which pained him more.

"Master!" said the Manservant, peering at him. "Master?"

Shielding his eyes so that only his Manservant could see them, the Fabulist used them to say, "Get in there, you idiot!"

The executioners seized the Manservant and thrust him into the cabinet. Three cranks later he emerged as the Fabulist had—cringing, shaking, and flinching at the world.

They were stripped of their clothes, a process that seemed to cause them as much pain as if it was their skin which was being peeled off. Then they were restrained against upright tables with little ties of softest yarn, which they claimed felt like iron straps cutting into their flesh. The Grand Inquisitor produced two goose feathers, and holding them up for the Fabulist and Manservant to squint at (for they had yet to open their eyes fully in the sunlight), he said, "May God bless these terrible instruments of torment, that by their dreadful work which yet is His work, they may slice through lies and perfidy and bring forth the truth." And with that he began to stroke the Fabulist's and Manservant's bare bellies with the feathers.

Oh, the cries of pain and mortal agony! Oh, the howls of suffering and anguish! At each stroke of a feather the Fabulist and Manservant split the air with their cries. These were so horrible and startling that many in the great crowd of Uaxalans could not look, despite having come out for blood. The Grand Inquisitor stroked the soles of the Fabulist's and Manservant's feet; he stroked their inner thighs and along the hairless undersides of their forearms; and their cries grew ever more bloodcurdling.

"Do you confess your crimes before God?" asked the Grand Inquisitor, but the Fabulist and Manservant went on shrieking and yowling, for with their eyes closed against the sun they could not be sure that the Grand Inquisitor was not continuing to stroke them somewhere.

"Do you confess?" the Grand Inquisitor again demanded.

"Fiend from Hell!" cried the Fabulist. "Do your worst!"

"In that case you leave us no choice," said the Grand Inquisitor. He snapped his fingers, and four of the prettiest palace handmaids appeared. Their long hair was golden; their skin was golden and smooth; and their splendid figures, plainly visible beneath their gossamer gowns, were bursting in all the right places with youthful vigor and plushness. They averted their eyes from the shocking nakedness of the Fabulist and

Manservant, and whispered together prettily.

"Handmaids," said the Grand Inquisitor, "your King now asks you to perform a special duty of vital importance for your country. And while this duty may be repugnant to you, especially in regard to the fat one here, be assured that your King would not ask it of you were it not completely essential. Nor should you be afraid that you will be doing anything improper or immoral, for everything you do today is consecrated by God through His officers here on earth. You may consider this platform one of His churches."

"But great sir," said the handmaids, glancing at the vast crowd, "even if this were a very large church, there would not be so many people watching."

"You are modest as befits you," said the Grand Inquisitor, "but we ask you to put aside your modesty just this once."

"Alas sir, we cannot," said the handmaids, giggling and blushing and huddling together.

"Do you love your Prince?" asked the Grand Inquisitor.

"Oh yes, sir—we do!" said the handmaids. "We love him more than you know!"

"Do you wish to see him again?"

"Yes we do!"

"Then do your duty, girls," said the Grand Inquisitor. "Do your duty."

Timidly, the four handmaids approached the Fabulist and Manservant, who had been observing them through slitted eyes. Now, as the handmaids drew near, their eyes grew wide, which the Uaxalans interpreted as signifying fear, but which, in reality, signified astonishment at just how comely the handmaids were. Never had the Fabulist or Manservant seen prettier girls; never had they smelled fresher skin; and never, as the handmaids went to work on them in pairs, had they felt more delicate or delicious caresses.

"Ohhh..." groaned the Fabulist.

"Ohhh..." groaned the Manservant.

"Excellent!" said the Grand Inquisitor, rubbing his hands together.

The handmaids shed their gowns (every man in the crowd of Uaxalans sighed), and gently they brushed their bodies against the bodies of the Fabulist and Manservant. The center of the Manservant's desire was now pointing at the sky, and even the Fabulist's, which had not shown signs of life since the birth of his youngest son, Ffrenchmullan, many years ago, began to stir and lift. "God in Heaven, help me to resist!" he cried.

"Your lips!" said the Grand Inquisitor to the handmaids. "Use your lips!"

Thus prompted, the handmaids planted kisses all over the Fabulist and Manservant, from ear lobe and neck to nipple and navel, and down to trembling twitching toes. They licked with their tongues like clinging wet velvet, and sucked or nibbled tenderly according to their individual lights. The cries that issued from the Fabulist and Manservant were indistinguishable from those they had produced as the Grand Inquisitor had stroked them with feathers; if anything, these cries were even louder. Yet as the Fabulist and Manservant were stirred to ever greater warmth in their expostulations (many of the Uaxalans could not help giving voice to their emotions, either), so too grew their apprehension that they would forget the role they were playing. Each tender touch brought them closer to tearing their hands from the yarn that bound them, and returning the handmaids' affections enthusiastically. The precariousness of their position caused the Fabulist to sweat and gasp for breath, and when the handmaidens attendant to the Manservant pushed their breasts into his mouth, smothering him in copious firm flesh, he felt as if he would expire. "Stop!" he begged. "It's more than a man can bear!"

And the handmaids had not yet even turned their attentions to their victims' most sensitive parts!

"Girls," said the Grand Inquisitor, his voice a husky whisper, "why do you delay?"

The handmaids looked solemnly at one another, to gird themselves, and then, obediently, they went south. First there were light strokings with a fingernail, from the pendant sack below, to the tip. Next came entwinings in the handmaids' long golden hair, which they swirled deliciously round and round. Then came thorough lickings, followed by deep swallowings which, in the case of the Manservant, were heroic inasmuch as his considerable size threatened to choke the handmaids, while the Fabulist caused barely a tickle in the back of the throat. Since the handmaids worked in pairs, while one was busy in the methods described above, the other was busy elsewhere with hands or mouth or breasts or bottom—and then they switched places so that neither might tire. In short, the handmaids did not miss a trick (many of which they had been taught by the Prince in long sessions), omitting neither thrustings between the breasts or ticklings of the nether muscle. Surely no sultan in his harem, no emperor among his concubines, no Bacchus at a bacchanal, nor even lucky castaway on an island of comely women had ever been treated to such painstaking attentions. The Fabulist and Manservant felt as if they *had* been sensitized, so overwhelming were their sensations. They moaned and groaned, howled and yowled, called upon the saints and archangels and denounced the handmaids as vile succubi, giving an altogether convincing impression of two men in most dire torment... which in fact they were. It was only their great fear of discovery that kept their volcanoes from erupting with flows of hot lava (so to speak).

And the handmaids had not yet even employed their sweetest portals!

The time had come. The Uaxalans grew silent, except of course for their heavy breathing. Even the King was aroused from inattention; he rolled his chair forward for a better look, and rubbed himself lewdly as if he were alone. The upright tables against which the Fabulist and Manservant leaned were lowered to horizontal, and the handmaids climbed up to straddle them. The Fabulist gulped as one of the handmaids poised her golden succulence above the capstone of his monument, which strained upward as though it would launch itself from his body. He closed his eyes, certain the game was over, and saw, to his great surprise, his wife's smiling face. At that moment, she seemed more beautiful to him than the handmaids, and the fact that he was about to be unfaithful to her, which he had never been throughout their long marriage, pained him more than the prospect of torture or death. He was filled with great sorrow. The Manservant, above whom a handmaid was similarly poised, must have had the identical thought, for he cried out weakly, "Forgive me, my love!"

As the mighty warrior is enraptured upon entering Valhalla, and as the worthy man is transported upon entering the gates of Heaven,

just so were the Fabulist and Manservant transported upon entering the handmaids.

"Mother of God!" exclaimed the Fabulist.

"Sweet Savior on the cross!" exclaimed the
Manservant. He gazed in wonder at the vision
that surmounted him; with a slow, exquisite
rhythm she subsumed and drew back, subsumed
and drew back, and he felt himself approaching a
final convulsion. His insides swelled beyond all
bounds, and then, with a stupendous arching
spasm, exploded into the girl. His arms flew up
and clasped her to him, and he shuddered
against her for what seemed, to him, like a period
much longer than his entire life to that moment.
He did not hear the Fabulist cry out, "No, man,
no!" Nor did he hear the Uaxalans gasp, nor see
their shocked expressions at his obvious pleasure.
He was lost in sensual ravishment; he felt a vast
unreasonable well-being; and he did what he
really ought not to have done, considering the
circumstances. He laughed in joyful release.

"A trick! It's a trick!" the crowd of Uaxalans
shouted, and they would have stormed the platform and pulled the Fabulist and Manservant to
pieces had not the King's Guard held them back.
The stunned handmaids were snatched away,
and the Fabulist and Manservant were snatched
from their tables and covered with cloaks.

The Grand Inquisitor stood before them. His
black eyes burned, and the points of his nose-hair

moustache twitched angrily up and down.

"So!" he said. "You make fools of us yet again!"

The Fabulist shrugged. "You can't blame us for trying," he said.

"Silence!" commanded the Grand Inquisitor, and he struck the Fabulist's cheek with the Uaxalan cross within rings within polygons. "And you," he said, turning to the Manservant, "you have debased us all with the spectacle of your filthy enjoyment!"

The handmaid who had received the Manservant's sum and substance, now in tears and clutching her gown against her violated body, ran forward and spat in his face. He dared not speak. He lowered his eyes shamefully, for he could not meet the Fabulist's.

"Very well!" said the Grand Inquisitor "Now you shall feel the full wrath of our nation. Good Uaxalans!" he called out. "What torture is foul enough for these foul persons, these evil adventurers, these contemptible, despicable—"

His voice was drowned out by the Uaxalans shouting their favorites: "The Boots! The Frying Pan! The Double Wheel!" and so forth. But soon one cry predominated, as more and more Uaxalans took it up until they chanted it with near unanimity, and this was: "The Barber of Blood!"

The Grand Inquisitor raised his hand and all fell silent. "Ah yes!" he said. "The Barber of

Blood! An excellent choice. How could I have forgotten?"

"The Barber of Blood?" asked the Fabulist. "What is that?"

"Not what, dog, but who," said the Grand Inquisitor. "And of this I am sure: there is no one else like him in the world. Fetch the Barber," he said to an executioner, who disappeared between the gibbets, gallows, racks, etc., which stood upon the platform like trees in a forest.

As all waited for him to return, the Manservant whispered to the Fabulist, "Oh, Master... I am sorry!"

"That's all right," said the Fabulist gently. "The temptation was beyond the human capacity to endure."

"But I have doomed us!" wept the Manservant.

"Don't blame yourself, for we wouldn't be in this dilemma if not for me."

"Of course, but—"

"To tell you the truth," said the Fabulist, "I had no idea what to do next, and we probably would have come to this pass anyway."

Just then the executioner led forward a shrunken, shambling, dirty old man.

"Now let us be as brave as we can," said the Fabulist to the Manservant, "and show them how men meet their fates."

The old man was greeted by great cheers and

shouts of encouragement, which caused him to look about in confusion.

"Good morning, Barber," said the Grand Inquisitor.

"What's that?" said the old man.

The Grand Inquisitor roared into his ear, "I said good morning!"

"Morning, is it?" said the old man, squinting at the sky.

"It is," shouted the Grand Inquisitor.

"Then why is it so damn dark?" the old man demanded. This caused the crowd to howl in delight, and the old man glared in that direction.

"But the sun is shining brightly," said the Grand Inquisitor.

"Am I inside somewheres then?" asked the old man.

"Why yes," said the Grand Inquisitor. "You are in a public house, and here are two gentlemen who wish to be barbered."

"I see," said the old man, though clearly he saw very little.

"Have you your implements?" asked the Grand Inquisitor.

"Of course," said the old man. He felt in the pockets of his dirty greasy smock, and drew out several straight razors whose blades were rusted, notched and cracked, and blackened with dry blood; also a large shears more suitable for hedges than hair; and a heavy iron tongs, for like most barbers he doubled as dentist. As he examined these tools with a professional eye—that is, he held them first at arms' length and then very close to his face, but without much satisfaction either way—the Fabulist and Manservant were pushed by executioners onto stools brought up from behind.

"I don't need a haircut," said the Manservant.

"Nor do I," said the Fabulist.

"Nonsense," said the Grand Inquisitor. "You want to look your best when you stand before God to be judged, do you not?"

"Aye!" shouted the wit from the crowd. "Take a little off the top!"

"But this is not a fit torture," said the Fabulist.

"True, it is a homely one," said the Grand Inquisitor, "but charming in its way."

"It is undignified."

"Bah!" cried the Grand Inquisitor. "Do you deserve dignity?"

"You are making fun of us in our extremity!"

"Oh, believe me, it will not be fun," said the Grand Inquisitor. "You have had all the fun you shall have." He turned to the Barber, but unnoticed during this little exchange, the old man had found his way to the King, once again oblivious in his chair, and assuming him to be the client, was aiming his razor at the Uaxalan monarch's shining dome, which he did not perceive was hairless.

"Stop him!" cried the Grand Inquisitor and the ministers, chancellors, viziers and wizards. An executioner caught the Barber of Blood's hand just as it began to descend. He was led back to the Fabulist and positioned on a box behind him. He stropped the razor on his legging, hocked up a yellow gob of spit upon it, and with his free hand felt for the Fabulist's head.

"A fine bush," he said. "How short?"

"Down to the neck!" someone yelled.

"Just a trim," the Fabulist said gloomily to the Barber. The barber raised the razor, and the Fabulist saw that his claw-like hand shook with palsy, and his eyes were milky with cataracts. Seizing a handful of the Fabulist's silver hair, he pulled it up ungently and began to hack away.

"Fine weather," he said amiably.

"Ow!" cried the Fabulist. "Be careful!"

"Where do ye hail from?" asked the Barber.

The Fabulist felt a burning atop his ear, and a bit of flesh dropped into his lap. "My God!" he cried, attempting to rise, but two executioners held him on the stool.

"Stop squirmin'," said the Barber, "or you might make me hand slip."

Soon the Fabulist looked like a badly cropped sheep, and he bled profusely from cuts and flayings all over his scalp. The Barber now resorted to his shears, scissoring up a long flap of skin that fell over the Fabulist's eye.

"Did I nick ye there?" asked the Barber. "Where's me styptic?" All this provided the Uaxalans with much hilarity, and opportunities for insensitive comment. The Manservant, however, gaped in horror at the Fabulist's worsening condition, while the Grand Inquisitor seemed quite interested in the blood that flowed freely down the Fabulist's face and neck. He dipped a finger in it, and sniffed it, but restrained himself from tasting.

"How's that?" the Barber said at last.

From the crowd came cries of, "Too long! Even it out!"

"Excellent," said the Grand Inquisitor.

"Thankee," said the Barber. "I may be old, but I'm still the best, you know. Ask anyone." He stepped down from the box and came around in front of the Fabulist. Brandishing the gore-caked razor in his face, he smiled and said, "Now then—how about a shave?"

The Grand Inquisitor's head appeared above the Barber of Blood's shoulder.

"Do you confess your crimes before God?" he asked the Fabulist.

The Fabulist was too miserable to hear.

"Do you confess your crimes before God?" the Grand Inquisitor said a second time, louder and more sternly.

"Caligulan!" spat the Fabulist between groans.

"For God's sake!" the Manservant begged the Fabulist. "Tell them something!"

"I will tell them," croaked the Fabulist, spraying blood that had run over his lips. "I will tell them to dive up my arse!"

"What's he say?" said the Barber.

"He said, why yes he'd like a shave," said the Grand Inquisitor.

It was not a pretty thing. The Barber's first stroke deprived the Fabulist of what remained of his ear; the second flipped his nose into the air. The Fabulist bellowed like an ox with each further whittling, so loudly that even the King looked up.

The Barber now palpated the Fabulist's throat in preparation.

"One moment," the Grand Inquisitor instructed. Then firmly he asked the Fabulist: "Where is the Prince?"

"On the island!" cried the Manservant.

The Grand Inquisitor demanded again of the Fabulist, "Where is the Prince?"

"In a whorehouse!" said the Manservant. "Joined an abbey!"

"*Where is he*?" roared the Grand Inquisitor.

"HERE!" rang a voice from the back of the square.

Many turned their heads in astonishment,

but the Grand Inquisitor had not heard over the agonizing of the Fabulist. "Where is the Prince?" he conjured fiercely. "*Where?*"

"HERE!" rang the voice again, and this time it was accompanied by girlish voices crying, "Here! The Prince is here! He is here!"

The crowd began to part at the rear, and like the wake of a boat this parting flowed swiftly toward the platform. The Uaxalans shouted, "The Prince? The Prince? Make way!"

And the voice that had rung out now thundered, "Stop! No more! Do not hurt him!"

"Hal?" said the King at the sound of this voice. He rose unsteadily from his invalid chair. "Is that my son?"

"The Prince?" said the ministers, chancellors, viziers and wizards, peering.

"The Prince?" said the crestfallen Grand Inquisitor.

"The Prince?" said the hopeful Manservant.

"Blub?" said the Fabulist, for with a final stroke the Barber had carved out his tongue.

"Father!" the Prince cried as he was lifted by many hands to the platform.

"Hal!" said the King, tears springing from his eyes. Invalid no longer, he ran toward the Prince who ran to him, and tenderly they embraced as the Uaxalans cheered terrifically.

"How? Where? What?" wept the King.

"Oh, Father!" said the Prince. "I've been such

a fool! Can you ever forgive me?"

"Forgive you? For what—for coming home?"

"For all the heartache I have caused you by my spoiled behavior…"

"Forgiven!" joyously cried the King.

"For thinking I knew everything and you knew nothing…"

"Forgiven!"

"For… for—oh Father, I nearly did the un-forgivable!"

"Not you! No surely… not you!"

"I would have," said the Prince, "if not for him!" He pointed at the Fabulist, and when the Prince saw up close the Fabulist's dire state, a gasp escaped him and he cried, "Sisters! Help me! Help *him!*"

The platform was flooded with Princesses in ragged remnants of once beautiful gowns, and in skirts of plaited fronds of palm. They clustered around the Fabulist and worked to stanch his wounds.

"This is the man I told you about, who saved your lives!" said the Prince, and the Princesses wept in gratitude, stroked the Fabulist lovingly and kissed away his blood. So tender and heart-felt were their ministrations that even through his great pain, and bewilderment at this sudden deliverance, the Fabulist could not help being put in mind once again of his Island of Comely Young Women.

"Wonderful man!" said the Prince.

"Gah?" said the Fabulist through bubbling blood.

"It was your story!" said the Prince. "Your story of the poor eyeless babies! I almost was too stupid to grasp its subtlety, but at last, among the pirates, I did!"

"Pirates?" said the King, glancing uncertainly at the Manservant. "I... I don't understand."

"Oh Father, there is so much to tell! But all will be explained to you—even the parts of which I am most ashamed."

"Do not forget the parts of which your father will be most proud," said Undine, who stood now on the platform.

"Undine!" said the King.

"Your Majesty," said Undine modestly, lowering her eyes.

"Seize her!" shouted the King to his Guard.

But the Prince intervened, "Father, no! She saved my life!"

"She? Saved *you*?"

"And he nearly gave his life for mine!" said Undine.

"Forgive her—forgive them all," said the Prince. "*I* have!"

"But Hal," said the King, "your mother!"

"We do her no honor by hatred and revenge," said the Prince.

"By God," marveled the King. "You *are*

changed!"

Blushing deeply, the Prince bowed his head. "I shall try to be changed," he said. "I feel that a black spot or blighting shadow has been lifted from my soul, and I shall try to live up to your example and mother's shining memory."

The King burst forth in fresh tears. "This is too good!" he cried, and throwing out his arms was smothered in Princesses. There were kisses and tearful *forgive-me's* all around, especially between the King, Prince and Fabulist, and even for the Manservant, who called each lovely Princess Blaise, after his daughter—and even on the part of the ministers, chancellors, viziers and wizards who hugged and huzzahed and congratulated one another (though the Grand Inquisitor's disappointment showed in the drooping of his moustache, and the Barber of Blood was much put out that no one had yet paid him for his excellent work).

Thus the platform that had begun as a stage for every possible form of painful death became now a theater of love overwhelming. Yet before we discretely draw the curtain on it and proceed to the epilogue to learn what became of our players over the next few days and the rest of their lives, let us eavesdrop for a moment on the Fabulist and Manservant, who came together in a little pocket of calm.

"Oh, sir," said the Manservant abjectly. "Last

night? That was no dream."

"Nug?" said the Fabulist, smiling.

"I'm so sorry!" said the Manservant. "I'm so ashamed!"

"Farb nozzle," said the Fabulist.

"But you are so good, so steadfast—so brave! You broke a solemn vow to try to save me! Oh you are better than I deserve!"

The Fabulist shrugged, as if to say, "Yes I am all that, but don't say you don't deserve me."

"If you can ever forgive—what I mean is— dare I ask it?" said the Manservant.

The Fabulist extended his hand, and the Manservant seized it. Yet the Fabulist frowned at his servile manner, and encouraged him with his eyes to be manly. And that was how they shook on things at the end of their adventure—man to man, not master to servant.

Epilogue

Because it was the fastest ship ever to fly over the tops of the waves, the *Bloody Doodle-Doo* was commissioned into the Royal Uaxalan Navy and ordered to return to the secret island as many times as necessary to fetch the rest of the King's wives and daughters, as there had not been room for them all when the Prince first returned to Uaxala in time to save the Fabulist. And because the Prince had destroyed the chart and only he knew the island's location, he was captain for these trips (besides, as slayer of Slag, who had more right than he?), and because the King could not bear to be parted from the Prince for an hour never mind days, he went along; and because the Princesses, who had crewed the ship under the Prince's command, had thought it such great fun, scampering up the ratlines as if they'd been born to it and seeming to know by instinct how to rig the tackles, work the cunt-splice, t'garns'l the sheets, and so on, they insisted on manning her again. In fact, they had gotten the sea in their blood, and this was the beginning of the famous Uaxalan Princess Marines.

As they sailed, the Prince told his father the full story of his misfortunes among the pirates and on the island, which to their amazement was exactly as the Manservant had recounted in the tower—except, of course, for how the Prince was nursed back to life by Undine and the others, as the Manservant had been interrupted before getting to that part.

Meanwhile, back in the palace, the Fabulist was attended by the King's own physicians, who fitted him with a silver nose and an exquisite silver ear like a shell. But there was nothing they could do for his tongue, so that the man who had been celebrated throughout the world as a teller of tales could no longer speak in an understandable fashion. Yet this did not seem to bother him; he seemed quite content to listen instead of talk. His eyes twinkled as everyone prattled on around him, and he made his few wants known by hand signals, or by writing on a slate which he wore on a silver chain around his neck. He was honored and banqueted by the Uaxalans as no one had been honored and banqueted before, and it was with difficulty that he was able to convince them that despite their kindness, he and his Manservant were really very anxious to go home. Only after accepting countless titles and distinctions, and exchanging weepy, deep-felt farewells

with the King and Prince, and promising some-
day to return (which they never did), were the
Fabulist and Manservant at last allowed to em-
bark with a crew of Princesses aboard the *Bloody
Doodle-Doo*. Therefore the voyage home, as op-
posed to the year-long voyage out, took only
three months, even though the ship was loaded
down with over-sized diamonds, double-
diamonds, black opals, heliotropes, sapphires,
tourmalines, peridots, rubies, innumerable other
gem stones and ingots of precious metals, with a
heavy Uaxalan Guard to guard it. The King also
wanted to send criers to proclaim the Fabulist's
greatness at length and in detail to anyone who
would listen, but the Fabulist would not allow it.

So much, then, for what happened immediately after the Glorious Reconciliation, as the
Uaxalans came to call the return of the Prince,
wives and Princesses. Let's move on to a quick
summary of the rest of our principals' lives.

The KING lived happily to an astounding old
age, and after his death the PRINCE ruled Uaxala
for many years as his father had: wisely, justly,
but most of all mercifully and compassionately,
as he knew his mother would have wished. He
took for his Queen one of Undine's daughters,
with whom he had fallen in love and she with
him as she tended him tenderly on the island,
and no one minded that they were half-brother
and half-sister, for that was how things were

done in those days and that place.

THE FABULIST, upon being reunited with his family, astonished them by his silverized appearance but even more so by his changed demeanor, which was thoughtful, self-effacing, generous, and concerned. He had much to make up for, but over time his wife came to accept him as a loving husband (who possessed the further advantage of having no tongue), and his children came to regard him as a devoted father and indulgent grandfather and great-grandfather. True to his vow, he never again told another fable or story or tale of any kind, and wouldn't have even if he'd been able to talk.

THE MANSERVANT, however, knighted and enriched by the Uaxalans and established with his family in a manor house of his own, took up the telling of tales, though not exactly where his former master had left off. It is his manuscript, which many have supposed to be invention but is true in every word, that you have just finished reading.

ABOUT THE AUTHOR

Joshua Landsman is no longer young, but is not yet old. He works at a job for a company. He lives in a suburb on the edge of a city. (You may have seen him.) He has done many things in life that he regrets, and a few things he is proud of. *The Tale of the Teller of Tales* is one of the latter.

"When Dwight Macdonald saw me, he said, I didn't imagine you looked like that. I think he was expecting a gnome." — *Harry Mathews, in* The Art of Fiction No. 191 *(Paris Review), on the reactions to his first book,* The Conversions.